Psychics

Fact or Fiction?

Other books in the Fact or Fiction? series:

Psychics

Fact or Fiction?

Tamara L. Roleff, *Book Editor*

Daniel Leone, *President*
Bonnie Szumski, *Publisher*
Scott Barbour, *Managing Editor*

OPPOSING
VIEWPOINTS®
SERIES

Greenhaven
Press®

THOMSON
GALE

San Diego • Detroit • New York • San Francisco • Cleveland
New Haven, Conn. • Waterville, Maine • London • Munich

THOMSON
—————*—————™
GALE

© 2003 by Greenhaven Press. Greenhaven Press is an imprint of The Gale Group, Inc.,
a division of Thomson Learning, Inc.

Greenhaven® and Thomson Learning™ are trademarks used herein under license.

For more information, contact
Greenhaven Press
27500 Drake Rd.
Farmington Hills, MI 48331-3535
Or you can visit our Internet site at http://www.gale.com

ALL RIGHTS RESERVED.
No part of this work covered by the copyright hereon may be reproduced or used in any form
or by any means—graphic, electronic, or mechanical, including photocopying, recording,
taping, Web distribution or information storage retrieval systems—without the written
permission of the publisher.

Every effort has been made to trace the owners of copyrighted material.

Cover credit: © Cameron/CORBIS

LIBRARY OF CONGRESS CATALOGING-IN-PUBLICATION DATA

Psychics / Tamara L. Roleff, book editor.
   p. cm. — (Fact or fiction)
Includes bibliographical references and index.
ISBN 0-7377-1125-6 (pbk. : alk. paper) — ISBN 0-7377-1126-4 (alk. paper)
   1. Psychic ability. I. Roleff, Tamara L., 1959– .

BF1031 .P794   2003
133.8—dc21   2002023619

Printed in the United States of America

133.8
Psy
$ 16.96

Contents

Foreword

"There are more things in heaven and earth, Horatio, than are dreamt of in your philosophy."
—William Shakespeare, *Hamlet*

"Extraordinary claims require extraordinary evidence."
—Carl Sagan, *The Demon Haunted World*

Almost every one of us has experienced something that we thought seemed mysterious and unexplainable. For example, have you ever known that someone was going to call you just before the phone rang? Or perhaps you have had a dream about something that later came true. Some people think these occurrences are signs of the paranormal. Others explain them as merely coincidence.

As the examples above show, mysteries of the paranormal ("beyond the normal") are common. For example, most towns have at least one place where inhabitants believe ghosts live. People report seeing strange lights in the sky that they believe are the spaceships of visitors from other planets. And scientists have been working for decades to discover the truth about sightings of mysterious creatures like Bigfoot and the Loch Ness monster.

There are also mysteries of magic and miracles. The two often share a connection. Many forms of magical belief are tied to religious belief. For example, many of the rituals and beliefs of the voodoo religion are viewed by outsiders as magical. These include such things as the alleged Haitian voodoo practice of turning people into zombies (the walking dead).

There are mysteries of history—events and places that have been recorded in history but that we still have questions about today. For example, was the great King Arthur a real king, or merely a legend? How, exactly, were the pyramids built? Historians continue to seek the answers to these questions.

Then, of course, there are mysteries of science. One such mystery is how humanity began. Although most scientists agree that it was through the long, slow process of evolution, indisputable proof has yet to be found.

Subjects like these are fascinating, in part because we do not know the whole truth about them. They are mysteries. And they are controversial—people hold very strong and opposing views about them.

How we go about sifting through information on such topics is the subject of every book in the Greenhaven Press series Fact or Fiction? Each anthology includes articles that present the main ideas favoring and challenging a given topic. The editor garners such material from a variety of sources, including scientific research, eyewitness accounts, and government reports. In addition, a final chapter gives readers tools to analyze the articles they read. With these tools, readers can sift through the information presented in the articles by applying the methods of hypothetical reasoning. Looking at these topics critically adds a unique aspect to the Fact or Fiction? series. Critical thinking can be applied to any topic to allow a reader to become more analytical about the material he or she encounters. While such reasoning may not solve the mystery of who is right or who is wrong, it can help the reader separate valid from invalid evidence relating to all topics and can be especially helpful in analyzing material where people disagree.

Introduction

Americans have a strong belief in psychic phenomena. A 2001 Gallup survey found that 50 percent of Americans believe in extrasensory perception and 54 percent believe in psychic healing. Just over one-third (36 percent) believe in telepathy, while just under one-third (32 percent) believe in clairvoyance, and 28 percent believe that people can communicate with the dead. The percentage of Americans who believe in these paranormal events has increased significantly—from 6 to 10 percent in almost every category—over the past decade.

Precognition

Along with the belief in paranormal phenomena, many Americans—including some famous Americans—claim that they have experienced some form of psychic activity. Abraham Lincoln told his friend and biographer Ward H. Lamon about a disturbing dream he had. In his dream, Lincoln heard loud sobbing and wailing. Following the sounds to the East Room of the White House, he had

> a sickening surprise. Before me was a catafalque [coffin-shaped structure] on which rested a corpse wrapped in funeral vestments. Around it were stationed soldiers who were acting as guards. . . . "Who is dead in the White House?" I demanded of the soldiers. "The president," was the answer; "he was killed by an assassin."[1]

Although he probably did not realize it, Lincoln's dream turned out to be precognitive, foretelling his own death.

Several days prior to Lincoln's assassination, Julia Grant,

wife of General Ulysses S. Grant, also experienced premonitions that something awful was about to happen. In response to her fears, she implored her husband to leave Washington and take them to their home in New Jersey. When a messenger sent by Mary Todd Lincoln arrived at the Grant home in Washington to ask the Grants to accompany her and her husband to Ford's Theater that night to see *Our American Cousin*, Julia Grant responded by saying they would be unable to attend because they were leaving the city that day. Then Julia sent several messages to her husband begging him to take them away from Washington that evening. As a result, the Grants were in Philadelphia when they heard that Lincoln had been killed. The news that John Wilkes Booth had also intended to assassinate General Grant, whom the papers had announced would be in the theater box with the Lincolns, confirmed that Julia Grant's fears were justified.

Precognitive dreams and premonitions like these are some of the most commonly reported psychic experiences. Other types of psychic powers include extrasensory perception (ESP), which in addition to precognition includes telepathy ("mind reading"), clairvoyance ("clear seeing"— seeing something in another time or place), and psychokinesis ("mind motion"—using the mind to make matter move, such as bending spoons). Out-of-body experiences, in which the body is left behind while a person's mind travels to another time or place, and psychic healing, in which the healer uses only his or her hands to perform surgery or cure diseases, are less commonly reported types of psychic ability.

Growing Interest

Interest in psychic phenomena—also known as psi—grew steadily in the second half of the nineteenth century. The spiritualism movement (based on the belief that the human spirit survives death and can communicate with the living) began in 1848 in the United States when two sisters from New York, Catherine and Margaretta Fox, maintained that they were able to communicate with the dead through rappings. The two sisters became famous and traveled from city to city giving demonstrations of their abilities to packed houses. They became professional mediums, and even though they later confessed that they had produced the rapping noises themselves, the public ignored and disbelieved their admissions of fraud and trickery. Soon, many others claimed that they were also able to call up spirits. In order to keep interest high, many mediums added table turning to their repertoire of psychic manifestations. Table turning—an event at which even extremely heavy tables would move across a room when a group of sitters placed their hands on the tabletop—replaced rapping as the favored paranormal phenomenon among mediums.

Table turning captured the interest of scientists, and this interest eventually led to the formation of an organization to study paranormal phenomena. In 1882, a group of respected scientists founded the Society for Psychical Research (SPR) in London. The society's stated purpose was to investigate "the large body of debatable phenomena designated by such terms as mesmeric, psychical and spiritualistic."[2] Three years later, the American Society for Psychical Research (ASPR) was founded in Boston. The SPR and the ASPR examined and researched many famous psychics and mediums in the late 1800s. However, the scientists—who were inexperienced at investigating paranormal phenomena—were often as easily fooled by their subjects as was the credulous public. Eventually, however, the researchers came to accept that the mediums they examined routinely used tricks and deceptions in their performances; still, a few mediums were believed to have genuine psychic powers.

One psychic medium who has not been exposed as a fraud is Daniel D. Home (pronounced Hume). Home was born in Scotland in 1833 and raised in Connecticut. He performed throughout the United States and England until his death in 1886. Among the phenomena witnessed at his séances were levitation (of himself, furniture, and other people), fire handling, rapping and other noises, strange moving lights, and musical instruments playing various melodies. Home was examined by two experienced investigators: William C. Bryant, a journalist and critic, and David Wells, a professor at Harvard. They attended a séance, inspected the room and furnishings, and examined Home himself. When they sat on a table during the séance, they felt it rise beneath them. Their report stated,

> While these men were so seated, the table started to move in various directions. After some time the table was seen to rise completely from the floor and floated about in the air during several seconds, as if something more solid than air was upholding it. . . . *We have the certainty that we were not imposed upon and neither were we the victims of optical illusions.*[3]

In fact, no report ever emerged that showed that Home was a fake.

The famous magician Harry Houdini desperately wanted to believe in psychic mediums, but his experience as a magician told him that most were frauds. He devoted much of his time to exposing the tricks and deceptions used by mediums. On the other hand, Houdini had little patience for scientific investigators. According to Houdini, "The fact that they are *scientists* does not endow them with an especial gift for selecting the particular sort of fraud used by mediums, nor does it bar them from being deceived."[4]

Opposing Houdini was an equally famous person: Sir Arthur Conan Doyle, the author of the Sherlock Holmes mysteries. Doyle was a staunch believer in mediums and spiritualism. Doyle so wanted to believe in spiritualism that he accepted as genuine many psychics whom others, such as Houdini and the noted psychic researcher J.B. Rhine, had exposed as fakes.

J.B. Rhine

J.B. Rhine and his wife, Louisa, had heard Doyle speak in 1922 in Chicago and were so impressed by his passion for spiritualism that they gave up their careers as botanists and took up parapsychology—the study of psychic phenomena. The Rhines attended a séance by noted medium Mira Crandon, who was known as Margery. Crandon was a favorite of Doyle's, and when the Rhines wrote to the ASPR stating that they believed her to be a fake, Doyle blasted them publicly. "J.B. Rhine is a monumental ass,"[5] Doyle wrote in a black-bordered advertisement in a Boston newspaper.

Despite such public condemnation of their opinion, the Rhines continued with their psychic research. They recognized that the biggest problem in studying a psychic phenomenon is that it is fleeting—it occurs once and then is gone forever, with no way to study it objectively. J.B. Rhine believed that the way to study the phenomenon he called "extrasensory perception" was to make it happen again and again. With this in mind, Rhine developed a deck of twenty-five cards with five different faces (known as Zener cards) to test ESP. His test subjects, using either guesses or ESP, would predict the face of each card. Chance alone dictated that five guesses out of the deck of twenty-five cards would be correct. Although an occasional subject might have more than five correct "hits," over a long series of tests Rhine predicted that the average amount of correct guesses would be 20 percent.

Rhine conducted 100,000 individual tests of ESP over three years before releasing his results in a monograph in 1934. The subjects in Rhine's study averaged 7.1 hits in each trial of twenty-five cards, an astounding average to keep up over such a large number of tests. Since his subjects scored significantly over the average of five correct hits per run, Rhine claimed that extrasensory perception was responsible. The odds that the results were due to chance are a googol (a one followed by one hundred zeros) to one.

Rhine's study drew all kinds of criticism from psychologists and other scientists. According to Richard S. Broughton, the director of research at the Institute of Parapsychology, critics condemned not only the research methods and statistics but parapsychology itself, "lest the enterprise reflect badly on orthodox psychology."[6] In response to the criticism, Rhine published another book, *Extra-Sensory Perception After Sixty Years*, a definitive report on ESP research since the founding of the SPR in 1882. Much to Rhine's surprise, Harvard University made *ESP-60* required reading in its introductory psychology classes in 1940. According to Broughton, SPR made psychic research a science, and Rhine gave it professionalism.

Ganzfeld Experiments

The next big development in psychic research was the ganzfeld (German for "whole field") experiment, developed by Charles Honorton in the early 1970s. Sensory deprivation is an important aspect of this experiment, for it allows the test subject (also called the receiver) to relax, clear the mind of "clutter," and focus on the experiment. Researchers had long noted that many psychic experiences occurred when the subject was meditating or completely relaxed. To facilitate such a relaxed state, the receiver sits in a recliner in a darkened, soundproof room. Each eye is covered with half of a Ping-Pong ball on which a red light is focused to produce a pink haze. A set of headphones provides some kind of steady sound, called white noise. In another soundproof room, a "sender" or "transmitter" opens a sealed envelope chosen at random. The envelope contains a picture, and the transmitter attempts to send that picture telepathically to the receiver. For thirty minutes, the receiver describes whatever images appear in his or her mind. After the session is over, the receiver is presented with the picture and three decoy pictures and asked to choose which one most closely resembles the one he or she envisioned. Then a transcript of the receiver's comments, along with the four pictures, is given to an independent judge who ranks how closely the pictures match the description. If the receiver's description and the judge's first choice of pictures closely resemble the target—the picture the transmitter was trying to send—a hit is registered.

For example, in a ganzfeld experiment conducted by British researcher Carl Sargent, the target was a black-and-white photo of firemen, their backs to the camera, holding hoses. On the photo's far left, however, was one fireman who was looking straight at the camera. The receiver's description was uncanny:

> Keep thinking of firemen and fire station. . . . Firemen definitely seen, black and white. People but not faces. I think one man at bottom in foreground, facing. . . . Young face as if photographer says, "Oi," and only he turned around.[7]

The receiver had no problem picking out the target photo, either.

In another experiment conducted by Honorton, the target was a video clip from the film *The Lathe of Horses*. In the clip, five horses were galloping in a snowstorm, then it showed a close-up of a horse trotting in a meadow, then the same horse trotting in city streets. The receiver easily picked out the target video clip:

> I keep going to the mountains. . . . It's snowing. . . . Moving again, this time to the left, spinning to the left. . . . Spinning. Like on a carousel, horses. Horses on a carousel, a circus.[8]

Honorton, Sargent, and other researchers recorded many similar hits in ganzfeld experiments.

The CIA and Remote Viewing

A psychic experiment that is similar in technique to ganzfeld is remote viewing. Remote viewing, a term coined by psychic researchers Russell Targ and Harold Puthoff, is also known as out-of-body travel. The subject relaxes, is given a place or time to visit, and with practice, leaves the physical body behind and goes to the site mentally. All the while, the subject is describing what is seen, heard, and felt at the remote location.

In the early 1970s, the CIA became concerned that remote viewing offered strategic and military advantages to the Soviet Union. In response, a remote viewing program was established in 1972 at Stanford Research Institute, now known as SRI International, to analyze the Soviet threat of espionage using psychic techniques. The Soviets had been conducting research in parapsychology since the 1920s when a preeminent Soviet researcher, Leonid Vasiliev, performed an experiment showing that telepathy could influence people over great distances. In the 1960s, the Soviets began studying the feasibility of using ESP to communicate with submerged submarines. The Soviet Union was responding to a newspaper article written in 1959 that wondered if telepathic experiments conducted by Bell Laboratories were being used to communicate with a submerged submarine, the USS *Nautilus*. In 1968, the Soviets reported that they had duplicated the *Nautilus* experiments and were building fourteen research institutes to study parapsychology.

These reports alarmed the United States, which, according to parapsychologist Elmar R. Gruber, "saw the investigations into 'mental suggestions' and 'remote influencing' in the context of 'telepathic remote control' and brainwashing, and [believed the] fear of the enemy superpower had been enriched by a new concrete threat, the 'mental attack.'"[9] It was imperative that the United States catch up to the Soviets in psychic research.

A 1972 report from the Defense Intelligence Agency stated why funding parapsychological experiments was so urgent:

> The major impetus behind the Soviet drive to harness the possible capabilities of telepathic communication, telekinetics and bionics [is] said to come from the Soviet military and the KGB. . . . Soviet efforts in the field of psi research, sooner or later, might enable them to do some of the following: (a) Know the contents of top secret U.S. documents, the movements of our troops and ships, and the location and nature of our military installations. (b) Mold the thoughts of key U.S. military and civilian leaders at a distance. (c) Cause the instant death of any U.S. official at a distance. (d) Disable, at a distance, U.S. military equipment of all types including spacecraft.[10]

According to Gruber, "Remote viewing was the U.S. answer to the Soviet psi threat."[11]

One of the most successful remote viewers used by the CIA was Pat Price, a former police commissioner and deputy mayor of Burbank, California. As a police officer, he had used his intuition several times to solve cases. Curious about his own powers, Price went to SRI to be tested for psychic ability. Targ and Puthoff found Price's psychic abilities extraordinary.

In Price's fourth trial at SRI, he astounded everyone with his declaration that he could describe the target destination before Puthoff, the sender, had even arrived there to send telepathic images back to Price. According to Targ, who tells the story in Miracles of Mind, Price said he "could just look 'down the time line' and see where they would wind up half an hour in the future!"[12] Price described the scene where he said Puthoff would later be:

What I am looking at is a little boat jetty, or a little boat dock along the Bay. . . . Yeah, I see little boats, some motor launches, some little sailing ships, sails all furled, some with their masts stepped, others are up. Little jetty, or a dock there. Funny thing—this just flashed in—kinda looks like a Chinese or Japanese pagoda effect. It's a definite feeling of oriental architecture that seems to be fairly adjacent to where they are.[13]

What made this test so astonishing to everyone at SRI was that Puthoff had no set destination in mind—a departure from the normal procedure—when he left the building. Puthoff decided that for this test he would drive aimlessly, guided only by his fancy and traffic. His target would be wherever he was a half-hour after setting out. Thirty minutes later, Puthoff stopped at a local marina. He gazed at the small sailboats bobbing in the water and looked at the marina's restaurant, which had a curved, sloping roof that made it look like a Japanese pagoda. What Puthoff did not know was that Price had completed his description of the site fifteen minutes before Puthoff arrived.

In another extraordinary test, Price spied on a Soviet installation in Semipalatinsk, Kazakhstan, that was thought to be a site for the development of atomic weapons. Price was given the coordinates of the site and began talking about and sketching what his mind saw. According to Targ, once Price mentally arrived at the site, he reported that he was

Lying on my back on the roof of a two- or three-story brick building. It's a sunny day. The sun feels good. There's the most amazing thing. There's a giant gantry crane moving back and forth over my head. . . . As I drift up in the air and look down, it seems to be riding on a track with one rail on each side of the building. I've never seen anything like that.[14]

Price's drawings of the compound were very similar to a drawing of the site the CIA made from a satellite photo.

The U.S. Army also began experimenting with remote

viewing in the late 1970s at Fort Meade, Maryland. The army's superstar remote viewer was Joe McMoneagle, a chief warrant officer. McMoneagle's most famous case was one in which he was asked in September 1979 to determine what the Soviets were doing in a large building in northern Russia. Satellite photos had shown heavy construction around the site, and the U.S. National Security Council wanted to know what was going on. McMoneagle was given the site's coordinates and asked to "look" inside the building there. He described and sketched a scene of a huge submarine still under construction, including how many intercontinental ballistic missiles it carried and its new drive and power mechanisms.

American authorities were skeptical of McMoneagle's assertion that a submarine was being built in the building: The alleged submarine was several hundred yards away from water, and the Soviets at that time did not have anything like the submarine being described. McMoneagle later recalled,

> Of course everyone disagreed with us. So I and another viewer from the unit produced a prediction that it would be launched on a specific date 112 days in the future. I believe we missed the date by three or four days. But, because of the prediction, they were able to watch the actual launch, which of course was an enormously successful operation.[15]

In order to launch the new submarine, the Soviets had blasted a channel from the building to the sea. At the time of its launch, it was the largest submarine ever built.

The army's funds for remote viewing ran out in 1985, and the project was taken over by the Defense Intelligence Agency (DIA). In 1995, the DIA tried to return the program to the CIA, but before it would accept it, the CIA insisted that the American Institutes for Research (AIR) evaluate the program. When the report—written by Ray Hyman, a preeminent skeptic regarding psychic phenomena, and Jessica Utts, a noted parapsychologist whose findings were overruled by Hyman—came back with a negative assessment of the program, the CIA publicly announced that it was officially terminating the up-till-then top-secret program.

Contemporary Research

Robert Jahn, a former NASA scientist and dean of the School of Engineering and Applied Sciences at Princeton University, founded a new program in 1979: the Princeton Engineering Anomalies Research Program (PEAR). The purpose of PEAR is to use sensitive machines to study micropsychokinesis—the effect the mind can have on a very small (micro) scale. Brenda Dunne, a psychologist at PEAR, explains the program this way:

> Gamblers throughout history have believed that they could affect the outcome of a random process like rolling dice or shuffling cards. The phenomenon we're measuring is a lot more subtle, but it's the same idea.[16]

PEAR uses a random-event generator (REG) in its tests of micropsychokinesis. (Random-number generators, or RNGs, are also used in these types of experiments.) Gruber explains how an REG works:

> An REG performs, on the micro level, the equivalent task of [the] tossing of a coin on the macro level. The REG produces "virtual" tosses of a coin in rapid succession. Depending on whether the coin comes up heads or tails, the number 0 or 1 . . . is shown.[17]

There are three types of tests the subjects, called operators, are asked to perform: The operators try to mentally influence the machine to produce either more 1s than 0s (aiming high), more 0s than 1s (aiming low), or to have no influence at all on the machine (to establish a baseline for the operator). Each trial consists of two hundred numbers (which are generated in under a second by the REG), so the laws of probability would dictate that each run, on average, would generate one hundred 1s and one hundred 0s. Jahn and his associates believe that any conclusions of REG research must be based on an extremely large database. In 1996, the PEAR lab had a database consisting of 1,262 series of experiments performed with 108 operators. Thirty of the operators had participated in 10,000 or more trials. Jahn, Princeton mathematician York H. Dobyns, and Dunne submitted a paper to the *Journal of Scientific Exploration* in which they had analyzed the 5.6 million individual tests and concluded that the operators' intentions do seem to affect the distribution of numbers.

Extraordinary Evidence

Skeptics argue that extraordinary claims of telepathy, clairvoyance, and remote viewing, for example, require extraordinary evidence before they will believe in such psychic phenomena. Without scientific proof that ESP and psychokinesis exist, critics assert that other explanations must be considered. Parapsychologists, however, contend that to simply reject paranormal phenomena without any consideration for their validity is itself unscientific. Most scholars and researchers have concluded that psi deserves to be studied, but in a scientific and rational manner. The authors of the viewpoints that follow present their arguments for accepting or rejecting belief in psychic powers.

Notes

1. Quoted in Time-Life Books, *Psychic Powers*. Alexandria, VA: Time-Life Books, 1987, p. 18.
2. Quoted in Richard S. Broughton, *Parapsychology: The Controversial Science*. New York: Ballantine Books, 1991, p. 63.
3. Quoted in Broughton, *Parapsychology*, pp. 61–62.
4. Quoted in Anthony North, *The Paranormal: A Guide to the Unexplained*. London: Blandford, 1996, p. 38.

5. Quoted in Time-Life Books, *Psychic Powers*, p. 50.

6. Broughton, *Parapsychology*, p. 71.

7. Quoted in North, *The Paranormal*, p. 167.

8. Quoted in Dean Radin, *The Conscious Universe: The Scientific Truth of Psychic Phenomena*. San Francisco: HarperEdge, 1997, p. 78.

9. Elmar R. Gruber, *Psychic Wars: Parapsychology in Espionage—and Beyond*. London: Blandford, 1999, p. 21.

10. Quoted in Gruber, *Psychic Wars*, pp. 21–22.

11. Gruber, *Psychic Wars*, p. 24.

12. Russell Targ and Jane Katra, *Miracles of Mind: Exploring Nonlocal Consciousness and Spiritual Healing*. Novato, CA: New World Library, 1998, p. 126.

13. Quoted in Targ and Katra, *Miracles of Mind*, p. 126.

14. Quoted in Targ and Katra, *Miracles of Mind*, p. 47.

15. Quoted in Gruber, *Psychic Wars*, p. 55.

16. Quoted in Gruber, *Psychic Wars*, p. 179.

17. Gruber, *Psychic Wars*, p. 178.

Chapter 1

Fact or Fiction?

Evidence in Support of Psychic Abilities

Scientific Experiments Suggest That Psi Exists

Hans J. Eysenck and Carl Sargent

Experiments using computers that display random numbers (called a random-number generator, or RNG) and illuminate lights in a random pattern (known as a random-event generator, or REG) show that psi exist, according to Hans J. Eysenck and Carl Sargent in the following selection. Test subjects recorded their guesses as to which number or light would be displayed next and the number of their correct answers were above what chance would predict. They assert that when the test subjects were asked to score below chance—to deliberately guess wrong—their answers were below what chance would predict. In experiments testing psychokinesis in which test subjects tried to get the lights to light up in a certain pattern, the authors report that their success rate was well above chance. When asked to score below chance, the subjects scored well below chance. Eysenck and Sargent conclude that these experiments suggest that

Excerpted from *Explaining the Unexplained: Mysteries of the Paranormal*, by Hans J. Eysenck and Carl Sargent (London: Prion, 1997). Copyright © by Hans J. Eysenck and Carl Sargent, 1982, 1993, and 1997. Reprinted with permission.

humans possess psychic ability. Eysenck is a psychologist. Sargent is a parapsychologist. They are the authors of *Explaining the Unexplained: Mysteries of the Paranormal.*

A German-born physicist, working 20 years ago for Boeing Research Laboratories in Seattle, was the first researcher to use [computer] technology to test psi in a thoroughgoing and systematic way. This man, Dr. Helmut Schmidt, devised an automated psi test machine which generated random numbers, registered subjects' guesses, and recorded all data in a form that was both easy to access and easy to process. With his machines, Schmidt hoped to conduct experiments which would eliminate errors of recording, inconsistencies of method, and other pitfalls.

Schmidt's research has furnished some of the most powerful evidence for psi yet recorded, and his work has also led to others duplicating his efforts. We will examine that subsequent research later, but first we need to understand the basic principles of his machines and test procedures. Obviously, over more than 20 years, these have developed and changed, but the basic principles remain much the same.

At the heart of Schmidt's psi-testing machines is a naturally occurring random process—the radioactive decay of the isotope Strontium-90. As atoms of Sr-90 decay, they emit rapidly moving electrons at random, wholly unpredictable, time intervals. The radioactive decay is detected and registered by a Geiger counter. In turn, the Geiger counter is linked to a very high-speed electronic oscillator. That oscillator cycles constantly between a number (usually four) of different electronic states, over and over. When the Geiger counter detects the emission of an electron, a counter driven by the oscillator stops, registering the state—

1, 2, 3 or 4—of the oscillator at the microsecond of emission. A simple visual display of numbered lamps allows one to see which state is being registered.

This set-up was used in much of Schmidt's work to test for precognition and psychokinesis. Subjects were asked to guess which of the numbered lamps would light next—a precognition experiment—or they were asked to concentrate on making one of the lamps light more than 25% of the time—a test for PK. The advantages of this kind of machine testing are clear. The test is simple and readily understood; the events to be predicted or controlled are truly random, and allow a clear measurement of subjects' successes in their psi tasks relative to chance; and the machine records results automatically, eliminating human error in recording (especially important in precognition tasks).

ESP and the Schmidt Machine

Schmidt published the results of his first ESP experiments in 1969. For these tests, subjects registered their guesses by pressing one of four numbered buttons. Pressing a button triggered the machine to produce a target which duly resulted in one of the four lamps being illuminated. The guess and the target (the lit lamp) were recorded on punched paper tape. The whole process, for one guess, was completed within half a second. To guard against cheating (or inadvertent error), the machine was constructed to ignore trials in which a subject pressed two or more buttons simultaneously, although if there were more than a millionth of a second delay between the pressing of two or more buttons, the machine automatically registered the first signal (pressed button) as the subject's guess.

Initially Schmidt tested some 100 subjects, drawn from Spiritualist communities and churches. He did this because he considered he might have his best chance of finding individuals with psi abilities among such people. He found one seemingly gifted individual, a doctor of physics, who was able to predict the behaviour of the machine to such an extent that the odds against chance for his performance were well over 100,000 to 1. Unfortunately, the man had to move away to a new job, so Schmidt was unable to test him further. However, the results persuaded Schmidt that the best approach would be to concentrate on a few gifted individuals.

Through further screening for people who appeared to have some ability, Schmidt selected three individuals for a formal experiment. All three had a strong interest in the paranormal. One was a male medium, another a teacher of 'psychic development', and the third, a truck driver, described himself as an 'amateur psychic'. Between them, they completed 63,066 guesses. The chance average score was, of course, 25%, or around 15,766 correct guesses, but the actual number of correct guesses was 16,458, nearly 700 more than chance would predict. While such a scoring rate was not very high (below 27%), because it was sustained over many thousands of guesses, the odds against it arising by chance exceeded 100 million to 1.

Schmidt began to vary his simple experiment by asking people to score high and low—asking them to use ESP to guess correctly and also to score below chance. This may seem perverse, but we'll be examining the often-reported phenomenon of 'negative ESP' or *psi-missing* later. Schmidt's medium was no longer available for testing, so this time he added the 16-year-old daughter of the truck driver as his third subject. When his subjects tried to score high they got just over 26% correct; when asked to score low, just below 24%. Again, the difference is small, but once more the odds are astronomical against this being due to chance.

Schmidt also conducted clairvoyance experiments. Here, targets were generated by the machine and stored on paper tape. The tape was then sealed inside the machine, which was then programmed to read off the tape and light lamps in the sequence corresponding to the tape. Instead of guessing future targets, his subjects had to guess targets already generated and stored—clairvoyance rather than precognition. Using his 'aim high, aim low' technique, Schmidt once again obtained results with odds against chance of around 250,000 to 1 from his expanding group of subjects (six in this study).

Checks and Safeguards

Before looking at some of Schmidt's other experiments, it would be useful to pause and consider the question of safeguards. Obviously, the results of Schmidt's early experiments were not due to chance. Could they have been due to some bias in the machinery? Well aware of this possibility, Schmidt made many checks. Since he had the punched paper record of all the guesses his subjects had made, in the original order, he could check if there was anything peculiar about any particular sequence which might have produced a distorted result. He fed the record of the guesses into the machine and checked it against an entirely new set of targets. The comparison showed a level of hits very close to 25%, well within chance expectation. Schmidt also regularly programmed his machines to produce long sequences of targets which he analyzed for bias. In an original series of over 5 million targets generated in this 'control' condition, and also in many later checks, there was no evidence of any patterning. The machine's output was wholly random. Neither statistical peculiarity nor mechanical bias appears remotely capable of explaining Schmidt's results.

Schmidt made other checks too. In one precognition study he used his machine as a recording device, but instead of using Sr-90 as the random event source he used a standard table of random numbers published by the RAND Corporation. In a 15,000-trial experiment, he obtained results well above chance (odds of 1 million to 1). Schmidt used machines constructed by himself and also by other workers at the Boeing Research Laboratories, and found that he obtained successful results independent of the machine type. His documentation contains details of these and many other checks.

PK and the Schmidt Machine

The combined results of Schmidt's ESP studies are impressive enough, but to these must be added some equally dramatic results from the PK experiments his later research increasingly focused on.

For his PK experiments Schmidt used a simplified version of his machine, with two (rather than four) output states. This is technically a *binary* (two-way) *random event generator*, or REG. This device was linked to a circle of lamps, with only one lamp being illuminated at any one moment. As the Sr-90 isotope emitted electrons, the REG converted them at random into negative or positive electrical pulses. When a pulse of one kind was delivered to the display, the currently lit light went out and the next one clockwise on the display lit up. Correspondingly, when the other type of pulse was delivered, the next counterclockwise light lit up instead.

The basic principle of Schmidt's machine remained unchanged. Instead of a box with four buttons and lights, the subject sees a clock-face of eight bulbs. In his PK tests, Schmidt instructed his subjects to sit quietly and try to 'will' the machine to generate pulses so that the lamps would 'jump' in a clockwise direction more often than in a counter-clockwise direction. If no PK effect is operating, the machine ought to take a 'random walk', with the direction of movement being equal in either direction.

In his initial experiment Schmidt found what appeared to be *psi-missing*: his subjects scored below chance. Schmidt selected the most consistent of his psi-missers and conducted a total of 32,768 trials (one trial being a single jump). With chance alone operating, the light ought to jump clockwise 50% of the time, but in Schmidt's experiment it did so just over 49% of the time. Again, the effect is small, but the odds against it being due to chance exceed 1,000 to 1.

While Schmidt has continued to report successful studies over the years, we cannot summarize all of them here, but four others (one by Schmidt, three by groups including Schmidt) deserve special mention. In the first of these Schmidt used a 'simple' REG (a binary system, as in the clock-face experiment) and also a much more complex one; this generated a large number of individual random events, computed how many there were of each type, and then presented the most commonly generated target to his subjects (this is the same principle as the majority-vote experiment with Stepanek, except that here it was applied to the target, not to the guesses). The scoring rate in this experiment was well beyond chance expectation (odds exceeding 100,000 to 1), and subjects scored the same rate of success on both machines. This is an important finding for understanding how psi might work. . . .

Robert Jahn's PK 'Operators'

Since [1982], a mass of reports has emanated from the Princeton Engineering Anomalies Research (PEAR) group at Princeton University. The head of the research group, Robert G. Jahn, is a scientist of unquestioned distinction, holding a prestigious post at a prestigious university. Like Schmidt, Jahn has used binary REGs and tested whether subjects can influence the outputs of these devices. And, like Schmidt, he has found that this indeed appears to be the case.

Jahn's research is formidable for any reviewer to deal with. The technical reports of the Princeton group are exhaustively documented, with data summaries which attain the size of telephone directories (fortunately, Jahn and his colleagues have written a summary book which is listed in the Bibliography). We cannot summarize all of the research here, but the key findings are readily appreciated.

Jahn's basic protocol uses both *volitional* and *instructed* tests. In a volitional test the subject decides which way he wants to 'will' the display to go, above or below a chance baseline level of scoring. Theoretically, this allows for either PK or precognition to occur. In an instructional test, subjects do not have free choice: the machine itself triggers a random event to determine which way they must try to use their will to influence its output. Also, Jahn's group runs machine control checks, including tests where the subjects (whom Jahn refers to as 'operators') are physically present and either ignore the machine's output or wish for nothing in particular to happen. This gives an empirical baseline condition, and the results from this are of as much interest as those where operators are actively intending to use PK.

The initial core of the Princeton data comes from experiments with rigidly fixed conditions (50 trials per run; a fixed number of samples—200—used to determine each trial outcome, like Schmidt's 'complex REG'; and predetermined numbers of runs per experiment). In experiments where subjects were asked to score above chance, they did so not 50% of the time (chance level) but 61% of the time. When asked to score below chance, they did so 64% of the time. Overall, the differences in scoring rate are very small. The scoring shifts from the chance average of 50% by a fraction of 1% only. But because the number of trials and runs is very, very large, the results are immensely statistically significant.

To appreciate the details of the results, it is important to realize that Jahn's group has not actively sought out people thought to have some special 'gift', as Schmidt did in his early research. However, the Princeton group has certainly reported results from one or two exceptional individuals who have come their way. Thus, from a first experiment with their now famous 'Operator 10', Jahn found that if asked to score above chance the man did so with odds against chance of 300 to 1; when asked to score below chance, he did so with odds against chance exceeding 100,000 to 1; and the difference between the two conditions was so large that the odds against that being due to chance exceed 3 million to 1. While the size of the possible PK effect is small, Jahn's results are no less statistically startling than those of Schmidt.

A really thought-provoking finding by Jahn is that operators have what he terms characteristic 'signatures' in the results of their experiments. Some can score above chance when asked to do so, but fail if asked to score below chance. Some show the reverse pattern. Others score above chance all the time, whether asked to score above or below. Different individuals show different patterns of apparent PK skill. The reason why this cannot be dismissed merely as a random collection of disparate patterns arising from chance variance is that the operators show relative consistency from one test to the next. Jahn is, in effect, reporting test-retest reliability for his subjects. Lump them together, even once one has excluded the exceptional subjects, and the overall results still show significant correlation with intention.

What is also intriguing is the result of the baseline series, as reported in 1987. From time to time a series of truly random events will throw up an exceptional result. This is the scatter effect. On average, once in every 20 experiments there will be a result which has a probability of 1 in 20, or .05.

Chance predicts this. What Jahn actually observed in 76 reported baseline series is *that not one* showed such a deviation. The machine output went on hugging the chance baseline in every case. This in itself is an unlikely event (probability around 1 in 50, not immensely small, but interesting). It is as if Jahn's operators were using PK to make the machine conform to chance during the baseline tests!

However, even eschewing such exotic possibilities, and even if we do the Princeton group a disservice by lumping all of their published research together, their work constitutes a really huge database—it comprises over 1.5 million trials. The effects are very small (a shift of only a fraction of 1% from chance expectation), but the overall odds against chance are over 20,000 to 1. In fact, this analysis does not do justice to the Princeton results because it obscures the different types of results obtained with different operators. Much larger anti-chance odds have been obtained in well-defined and controlled experiments with particular individuals who have produced databases of many tens of thousands of trials. . . .

We are not aware of any significant critique of Jahn's work other than the scrutiny of the National Research Council, or NRC, . . . (at this stage we will merely observe that it is a fiercely criticized document). Indeed, critical attention to the Jahn group's research has been a fairly limp effort. Here is a sample, from Victor Stenger's book *Physics and Psychics*. 'I can only speculate, and again I must make it clear that this is not an accusation of fraud, just a critical examination of the possibilities. Electronic circuits are known to "drift". They are often sensitive to heat, shock and humidity. Perhaps the operator noticed a drift over the weeks, and took advantage of it. Perhaps she simply kicked the apparatus, turned it upside down, or blew on some of the transistors.'

Such remarks hardly qualify as 'critical examination'. The

conditions of Jahn's experiments simply do not allow the kind of tampering suggested, especially since a larger body of remote experiments, generated under double-blind conditions, with the operators up to several thousand miles away from the machine while it was running, produced significant results similar to those of local experiments. The contrast of high- and low-scoring conditions eliminates the drift possibility (which is also specifically excluded by the counting circuitry of the device and confirmed by ongoing calibrations). Again, the curious reader should consult Jahn's original reports (see Bibliography). We can assure the reader that the kind of criticism quoted above makes an interesting comparison with the quality of Jahn's own documentation.

Perhaps such lackadaisical criticism is motivated by the fact that the effects in Jahn's studies are typically so small. We have already addressed that issue, but a final point might be noted. Quantum physics also deals with effects which are sometimes incredibly hard to detect. Trapping neutrinos, for example, requires very expensive equipment and a great deal of waiting time. The effects in this branch of science are sometimes so fleeting as to make Jahn's effects look highly robust by comparison! . . .

Towards a Broader Base of Evidence

We have looked at . . . the work of two research laboratories on machine PK. Our conclusion is that these sources of evidence form a strong basis for considering that human beings may possess some kind of faculty or ability which allows them to sense, and act, in ways which do not accord with the known 'laws' of physics.

Bibliography

Schmidt's simplest REG system is described in his article 'Anomalous prediction of quantum processes by some human subjects', Boeing Scientific Research Laboratories Document DI.82.0821. Schmidt has published many articles in *Journal of Parapsychology* (his first report appeared in 1969, vol. 33, pages 91–108) and *Journal of the American Society for Psychical Research* in the last 25 years. The research of the Jahn group is summarized in R.G. Jahn and B.J. Dunne, *Margins of Reality* (Harcourt Brace Jovanovich, 1987). The technical bulletins of the PEAR group are not easily available, but this book gives abundant detail. Dean Radin and Jessica Utts' paper is in *Journal of Scientific Exploration* (1989, vol. 1, pages 65–79).

Psychic Mediums Can Communicate with the Dead

John Edward

John Edward, host of a syndicated show, *Crossing Over with John Edward,* and author of *One Last Time: A Psychic Medium Speaks to Those We Have Loved and Lost,* is a psychic medium. The following viewpoint is an excerpt from Edward's book *One Last Time: A Psychic Medium Speaks to Those We Have Loved and Lost.* Edward asserts that he is able to communicate with people who have "crossed over" by connecting with the spirit's energy. Edward receives mental messages through sounds, images, thoughts, and feelings that he contends are put into his mind by spirits. He maintains that providing facts about either the person who has passed on or their loved ones left behind is proof that he is actually communicating with the dead. He gives several examples of readings that he has done for clients and what the messages he received meant.

Excerpted from *One Last Time: A Psychic Medium Speaks to Those We Have Loved and Lost,* by John Edward (New York: Berkley Books, 1998). Copyright © 1998 by John Edward. Reprinted by permission of Berkley Publishing Group, a division of Penguin Putnam Inc.

I want you to know how I do what I do. Of course, it's very difficult to explain in any kind of scientific way, so maybe a better way to put it is to say that I want you to know *what* I do—beyond simply saying I talk to the dead. Like other psychics and mediums, I hear sounds, see images, and—the most difficult to explain—feel thoughts and sensations that are put into my mind and body by spirits on the Other Side. They do this in order to convey messages to people they have left behind on the physical plane.

Psychic Sign Language

In some cases, I can give a good reading simply by passing on what I'm hearing, seeing, and feeling. But in most instances, I must interpret the information so that the meaning is understood. I call the entire process "psychic sign language." What I've been able to do in the years since I started this work is to become more fluent in understanding the symbols, making it easier for me to validate the presence of spirits. And ultimately, that is one of their chief goals: to convey enough specific, irrefutable information to prove that this is real and that they are actually still here with us, albeit not physically. Once they've done that, they've gone a long way toward achieving their greater purpose: making those of us on this side understand that they did not disappear into some black hole of nonexistence when they "died," but that they have only passed into another form—as we all will someday. They communicate with us not only to let us know they are fine—as we will also be when we get there—but to assure us that they are still involved in our lives, whether it's by acknowledging a birth of a baby or by remarking that they like a new hairstyle.

All of us—we in physical bodies and those in the spirit world—are made up of energy expressed as atoms and molecules spinning and vibrating at certain speeds. The energy of spirits vibrates at a very high rate, while ours goes much slower because we are in physical bodies. How we bridge the gap dictates how well communications traverse these two dimensions. That's the job of a medium.

For spirits to come through, they must slow their vibrational rate of energy. Think of the blades on a helicopter. You can't see that there are four of them because they are spinning too fast. That's how I view the energy of the spirits. What happens during a reading is that as the spirits slow down their energies, I speed mine up. Communication is what happens in that space in between. But because there is that space, that gap, communication is never easy and rarely clear. There is also the fact that spirits no longer have physical bodies to facilitate communication. They have no tongues or vocal cords to pronounce words. Instead, through their energies, they place thoughts and sights and sounds in my mind. I am their mouthpiece. Though I expected to hear a great voice from beyond when I first started this work, I soon realized that it is my own voice I hear—but their thoughts and feelings.

Because both sides must expend so much energy to make this happen, the communication is very difficult and can't be sustained for more than a few minutes. To switch metaphors, it's as if you have to go to the bottom of a twelve-foot-deep swimming pool to meet your loved one. You can do it, but it takes a lot of energy to get there and after a few seconds, you have to float back to the top for air.

So how does it happen? While it's true that I naturally attract the energies of spirits—they know I can perceive, understand, and convey their meaning—I make sure I do everything possible to maximize that ability. To do this, I go through a series of exercises to raise my vibrations to meet those of the spirits.

First, I meditate. I center myself so that my energies are as focused as they can be. As a Catholic, I also pray the rosary; I pray that I will be able to deliver messages clearly and that people will be receptive to those messages. I started doing this after many spirits showed me rosary beads turning into musical notes, a symbolic message that the rosary (and any intense and repetitious prayer, whatever one's faith) is almost literally music to their ears. It brings us closer to them, and them closer to us. Everyone has the ability to receive these energies to some degree. What I have is the ability to look at them with a different set of eyes, feel them with a different set of hands, and listen to them with a different set of ears than most people.

Psychic Senses

It is not a conversational language, though many believe it is. When I do a reading, people might think I'm repeating exactly what I'm hearing. But what I am actually doing is delivering and interpreting symbolic information as fast as I can keep up with it. If it were truly conversational, I would be a lot more accurate than I am. It's just not that simple. Rather than just talking and listening, the tools of my trade are my psychic senses. Just as we use the five basic human senses—sight, sound, touch, smell, and taste—a medium uses the same basic senses, only psychically.

Here is a description of each of these senses:

Clairaudience (clear hearing)—I am able to hear sounds, including voices, that come from the spirits. Mostly, I hear my own voice—my mind's voice—rather than the voice of the person whose spirit is coming through, though I have on occasion heard messages from a male, female, or even my mother's voice. Imagine that while you are reading this you are also thinking about whether or not you left the oven on. That's your mind's voice. That's how spirit messages sound to me.

Clairvoyance (clear seeing)—This allows spirits to show me objects, symbols, and scenes. Sometimes these are meant literally, as in the image of a car to convey to me that the spirit passed in a car accident. Other times the image is more symbolic. That same car might be shown to me as a symbol of something else. For example, a spirit might show me a Ford to get me to say that name. And to use the example above about thinking about whether you turned the oven off, your mind might show you the oven. That's how I see these images. Clairvoyance is also how spirits show me what they looked like while in the physical body, either by showing me themselves or someone I can identify who fits the same description.

Clairsentience (clear sensing)—This is feeling or sensing a spirit's message. This can take a variety of forms. It's how spirits convey emotions they felt or are feeling, as well as physical feelings to show me what they were feeling prior to death and after. This sometimes includes "sympathetic pain," where I "feel" what parts of their physical bodies were the focus of whatever problems they had. Through clairsentience I have felt chest pains, stomach pains, joint pains. In other cases I have felt emotions ranging from love to sorrow.

Clairalience (clear smelling) and clairhambience (clear tasting)—I get smells and tastes that help me convey validating messages. Clairalience is sometimes referred to by mediums as "smelling them," whether it be a perfume, a cigar, or some other scent closely associated with the person now in spirit.

Interpreting the Message

A good reading depends on my using all these senses at once, putting together the various symbols, sounds, and feelings and interpreting them into a coherent message. This is why my work can be extremely draining. It may seem as if I'm just sitting there pulling things out of the air and relating them, but my brain is working hard, trying to catch what can be a bombardment of thoughts and images and interpret them.

Some things, of course, are easily interpreted. Names, for instance. As long as I am hearing it correctly, there's no doubt what it means. It's either the name of the spirit, or that of someone the spirit is acknowledging. The trick is distinguishing between the two. Sometimes the spirit will help by giving me, for instance, a feeling of going up to indicate someone in the generations above: parents, grandparents, aunts, uncles. Or a parallel feeling, to the side of the client, if I am meant to convey a brother or sister, a cousin, or a friend. To indicate a child, the spirit will focus my energies downward. It's one example of clairsentience.

Oftentimes, I get a combination of feelings that I use to decipher the identity of either the spirit or the person the spirit is referring to. A lighter, softer feeling tends to indicate a female, while a stronger, dominant presence indicates a male. (There are, of course, exceptions in the cases of men who come through more gently and women who are strong and dominant.)

In each case, I will tell the client what I am feeling to make it easier for him or her to identify the spirit. Sometimes I use the client as a guide. "Tom was my brother," he might say, giving the reading an early context by indicating that Tom is the one coming through. But other times, the *spirit* will be the guide. For example, if my client says, "Tom was my brother," I might say, "Okay, but this is a different Tom, because he's definitely showing me he's above you on the family tree."

Besides those of people, I have heard all kinds of names—

of places, songs, movies. I also hear phrases. But the clarity varies wildly. Very few things come in loud and clear, as if they've been handed to me in lightning bolts on a tablet and I can just read it: *This just in from the Other Side.* Clairaudience means "clear hearing," but in reality it is far from that.

With names, for instance, sometimes I get the whole thing, other times just an initial or a sound. Sometimes it's analogous to a radio with very heavy static. You hear a voice, but it's not clear and you try to catch a word here or there. Other times the messages are very faint, like a whisper, or come and go incredibly fast. You catch it for a split second as it rushes by, like a train. And still other times it's like a voice that keeps breaking up. If a spirit were to try to give me the name James, I might just get the "J" sound or a "J-S" sound. "Ellen" might come through with the "L" sound strongest, or "L-N." By experience, I would probably know that the spirit is not giving an "L" initial, indicating it's a name that begins with that letter, but that it's the dominant sound. So I would give that as Ellen or Ellie or some variation. "Oscar" would come through as an "S," the dominant sound. With experience, I have become sharper at picking the names out, better at differentiating between, say, "Ellen" and "Helen," or between "Jack" and "Jacques." I might be off on the full name, but I virtually always get the initial or the sound. Over the years I've been able to turn up the volume, but that hasn't made it any easier to understand the messages. If there was one thing I would ask the spirits, it would be to slow down and speak more clearly.

Images

Images are next on the scale of difficulty, but for a different reason. It's not that I don't see them well, but that they are often meant symbolically and it's up to me (with the help of my client, who knows what the big picture looks like) to figure out what they mean. Some things are like stock images: I'll be shown a white rose to indicate congratulations for an upcoming birthday or celebration. A red rose marks an anniversary of a wedding or death. Parallel lines indicate there's a parallel between the spirit and the person I am reading or, depending on the context, someone else. For instance, if they look alike, have the same name, or share some similarity or interest.

Some images are easy to interpret. I have been shown Mickey Mouse to indicate there was a trip to Disneyworld. A badge might symbolize something to do with law enforcement. Diseases are even more literal. If I'm shown blood circulating through a body, for instance, it usually means the person passed of a blood disorder such as leukemia or AIDS, or, depending on what else I'm getting, that the person sitting in front of me has such a disease affecting the bloodstream. Black spots on a part of the body indicate cancer.

Because errors in interpretation are the most common problem in readings, I sometimes try too hard to get it right and wind up overinterpreting. As the saying goes, sometimes a cigar is just a cigar. During one reading, a woman's husband came through strong and clear. He gave me many details that his widow confirmed as accurate. The reading was like a gift; I felt like I was hardly working. But throughout the session, I kept getting an image whose meaning I couldn't pin down. It was a bell. What could this mean? I started throwing out possibilities to my client: Liberty Bell, Philadelphia, Ben Franklin, Betsy Ross, Colonial America. The woman kept shaking her head and saying no. Finally, almost in desperation, I said, "He's showing me a bell. Do you know what he means?" She froze and gasped. I saw tears forming. She took a deep breath and told me that her husband had gone on a business trip and brought home a souvenir bell but had forgotten to give it to her when he came home. Getting ready for work the following Monday morning, he saw the bell in his briefcase, walked back into the bedroom, and rang it. "If you ever need me, ring this and I'll be there," he said with a smile. He put the bell on the night table and kissed his wife good-bye. He was killed in an accident on the way to work. Sometimes a bell means . . . a bell.

Spirits love to show me numbers. Barely a reading goes by without my seeing at least a couple, though their meaning is often vague. If I'm shown the number 7, for instance, it could mean something significant happened in July, the seventh month, or on the seventh of a month. Or even that it happened seven months ago or seven years ago. And there are times when it's not clear what that significant event is. It could be a birth. It could be a death. So the number will only be a small piece in the puzzle: it only has meaning when put together with other information.

In many cases, spirits will show me things I will relate to but which are meant to represent something else to the person I'm reading. For instance, I'm often shown my own car. It might mean that the spirit passed over in a car accident. It might mean he sold cars for a living. It might mean that the person I'm reading is now driving the car of the person who has passed. I often need the client to help me pin this down.

Spirits give me messages in part by knowing what I will understand. Their genius is in using a combination of human logic and spiritual energy to put the right images in my head. It's as if they're saying, "How can we get him to say this?" My brain is their file cabinet, and my life experiences are the files and folders inside that cabinet. Or to give it a more modern analogy, it's as if the spirits have a personal computer on which they can type in a message they want to convey and up on their screen will pop the best way to get that message across. For me, pop culture references are common: TV shows, movies, Broadway shows. Shelley Peck once told me, "John, I wish I knew as much TV as you do. It would make it so much easier."

Frustrations

But then, sometimes it just complicates matters, especially if I try to interpret information rather than telling a client exactly what I'm being shown. One tough night, I kept telling a woman who had lost her husband that "Kim" or "Kimberly" was being acknowledged. I based this on the spirit showing me Kim Zimmer, an actress who plays a character on the soap opera *Guiding Light.* But he wasn't acknowledging anyone named Kim at all. He was trying to show me how he had died. He showed me Kim Zimmer's character jumping off a bridge. This was how he had died.

This is what can happen when a spirit is not adept at communicating or a medium is not clear about what he is receiving. It can be an extremely frustrating experience for all concerned. It's why I stress that not every reading yields solid, detailed information that leaves a client floating on air. It can be vague, confusing, and disappointing.

In a good reading, I will get images that are specific to a person or a family, and are meant more literally. I once had a spirit come through showing me a bowl of spaghetti with raisins in it. It's all the confirmation her daughter needed. That's how her mother made spaghetti, every Sunday. How many people put raisins on spaghetti? No one in my Italian family. . . .

Clairsentience

Clairsentience is the hardest to describe because it's more a *feeling* than anything else. I'm not seeing or hearing it, but it's around me, as if I'm somehow *wearing* the feeling. Unlike with the other senses, it also tends to hang around, rather than whizzing by me. And if I'm not getting it right, the feeling will start to feel bigger and bigger until I do. In that sense, it is a living, breathing experience, with spirits responding to me, trying as hard as I am to bring the messages through.

Clairsentience often takes the form of an attempt to put me into the body a spirit had before passing to the Other Side, literally making me feel something of what they felt, giving me information that will validate their presence. A feeling of being hit over the head would indicate a blunt trauma, either in an accident or a homicide. A pain in the stomach might indicate stomach cancer. Other feelings are more subtle. A suicide will come through to me with the feeling that a person brought about his own death. But this is tricky ground because I will get a similar feeling for someone who caused his own death unintentionally. (Obviously, I have to be careful when conveying this to clients.) . . .

More often, I am given feelings of peace and love, because that is the most important thing they are trying to get across. Many times this happens in cases where a sense of guilt is involved. For instance, when a client feels guilty about not having taken an action he or she thinks might have saved the life of a loved one. Or guilt that he never said good-bye or made peace or said, "I love you." In cases like this, a spirit will often give me a feeling of great release, as if I'm suddenly let go from something. I interpret this to mean that the spirit wants me to say to the person, "Don't feel guilty. I'm okay."

On occasion, I have also been imbued with extraordinarily strong feelings of love. In these cases, which are unfortunately not that common, spirits have conveyed their love for someone I am reading by making *me* feel love for that person—someone I have never met before and will probably never see again. It comes out of nowhere. I'll be in the middle of saying something, then I start to feel a warm sensation come over me. It's as if I am at the shore, submerged in about a foot of water, and warm waves are washing over me. That spirits can seemingly get inside our brains and bodies and superimpose such images, thoughts, and feelings is the magic of the spirit world. It is as hard to rationalize as it is to explain a sunset. . . .

I like to think of psychic energy as akin to radio waves. Even without the radio on, the air is filled with invisible signals from countless radio stations operating on their various frequencies. All you have to do to receive them is to flick the radio on and tune the dial. When I do a reading, I flick on my own switch and wait for the program to come on. And if I miss a message, they have been known to turn up the volume.

The frustration, especially in cases where obscure information flashes by quickly, is that my client can't see what I'm seeing or hear what I'm hearing. Here's some science fiction: Maybe someday there will be some kind of psychic virtual reality, where I could hook myself up to a screen and a pair of speakers, describe what I'm receiving and have the client see and hear it at the same time, maybe even feel it, especially the overwhelming feeling of love that I get. That's my dream, but until then, we'll have to settle for this less than perfect system.

Psychic Detectives Help Police Solve Crimes

Charles E. Sellier and Joe Meier

Charles E. Sellier is a writer, TV and film producer, and chairman of Sun International Pictures in Salt Lake City, Utah. Joe Meier is also a TV writer and coauthor of several books with Sellier, including *Miracles and Other Wonders* and *The Paranormal Sourcebook: A Complete Guide to All Things Otherworldly*. In the following viewpoint, they observed several psychic detectives help police solve crimes. The psychic detectives operate in several different ways, they report. Some are able to "see" the crime and the criminal by holding objects associated with the crime. Others are haunted by vivid dreams of the crime. Some psychics are able to perceive images just by talking with the police detectives in charge of the case. However, the authors note that psychic detectives are not always believed by the police, and some psychics have even been considered suspects because of their knowledge of the crime. While not all their predic-

Excerpted from *The Paranormal Sourcebook: A Complete Guide to All Things Otherworldly*, by Charles E. Sellier and Joe Meier (Lincolnwood, IL: Lowell House, 1999). Copyright © 1999 by Lowell House. Reprinted with permission.

tions are accurate, Sellier and Meier find it is amazing, given the circumstances under which they work, that psychics are able to help the police at all.

The Los Angeles Police Department had very quietly been using psychics for some time before I called and asked them if we could film one of their psychic detectives in action. To my surprise, they were cordial and accommodating. My surprise stemmed from the fact that they knew we were making a motion picture, and I would have thought that their use of psychics would be something they would want to keep secret.

The World's Most Famous Psychic Detective

What the police knew that I didn't was that we would be filming the work of a young man by the name of Peter Hurkos, whose stunning accuracy had been proven several times before. They were confident that Peter would come through for them again, even with the cameras rolling.

Peter Hurkos is today the world's most famous psychic detective. Indeed, the term may originally have been coined to describe him. At the time of our meeting, however, he was just one of several psychics that the LAPD used, although he was their most accurate in terms of crime-solving success.

We were invited to go to Peter's home. The arrangement was that we could set up our equipment, lights, sound, cameras, everything, just like a regular shoot, but we had to remain quiet and in the background. We were instructed to do nothing to attract attention to ourselves. The case that Peter would be working on was a multiple murder, and the police had only one clue for him to work with.

When everything was set up and ready to go, I moved to

the background and settled in to watch. My earlier experience with Uri Geller had taught me not to prejudge these people, but I was not prepared for what happened next.

A police officer came into the room. In his hands he was carrying something wrapped in a scarf. Peter was sitting in a large, overstuffed chair, still trying to get comfortable with the lights and equipment even though it was well back and out of the way. As the officer approached, Peter suddenly became very agitated. The officer had not yet unwrapped whatever he was carrying, but it was clear that Peter found it disturbing.

"You're carrying a bloody knife," he said, pointing at the scarf.

The officer nodded silently and handed the knife, still completely wrapped, to Peter. Hurkos stiffened, almost as if he had been struck with an electric shock. Sweat began to pour from his face and forehead. His hands shook as he opened up the scarf and revealed the bloody knife.

At this point, the words began to rush from his mouth, and as the information poured forth, his whole body seemed to get involved. First he described, in great detail, the room where the knife had been found. He told the officers (and our cameras) where the windows were, where every chair was in the room, even what could be seen from the windows. Then he began to describe each person who had been in the room when the murders took place. He gave a detailed description not only of what they looked like, but how they were killed. All of this, we were assured by the police, was in complete agreement with what they already knew, even though Peter had been given no information about the case beforehand and in fact didn't even know the nature of the crime until he was handed the bloody knife.

Then the really remarkable portion of the session began. Peter began describing the *feelings* of the killer. Hurkos seemed to be able to insinuate himself into the murderer's mind. He told the police what the killer was thinking at the moment of the crime and how he felt inside when the deed was done. But he didn't stop there. Peter gave the officers considerable detail about the place where they might find the killer, and finally, he gave them a physical description of the man.

I stood in open-mouthed amazement as the information poured out. It was almost as if he were reading from a book. There were few hesitations and no equivocation about anything. Three weeks later, the LAPD made an arrest in the case. The killer matched Peter's description in every important detail.

Following the arrest, we went back and interviewed one of the officers. He admitted that the reason they had gone to Hurkos in the first place was because, other than the murder weapon, they had no leads at all: no fingerprints, no witnesses; they literally didn't have a clue. Somehow, by simply holding the murder weapon, Peter had been able to lead them to the killer. The officer, who had worked with Hurkos before, seemed almost blasé about it, but to me it was one of the most impressive exhibitions of psychic power I had ever seen.

In the years that followed, Peter Hurkos's fame spread worldwide, helped in no small way, I'm sure, by our film. We had opened the door just a crack on something that police departments had been doing for some time (the LAPD was by no means the only police department using psychics). The secrecy was not due to any lack of success, but rather to an understanding of human nature. Even now, there are those of you reading this book who are saying to yourself, "I don't believe it." Unfortunately, for a significant number of criminals, many police departments did and still do "believe."

Peter Hurkos was an intentional seer and went on to not only fame, but a certain degree of fortune as well. That is not always the case, of course, and some psychic detectives have come to regret even one vision of a crime.

Haunted by a Dream

Approximately twenty years ago, Judy Jones (not her real name) was jolted awake one night by a dream so real that every detail remained with her long after she was awake. She tried desperately to make it go away, but to no avail. What she had seen was the body of a young woman being dumped somewhere in a wooded canyon. The terrain in the area surrounding her home included several small canyons, but they were fairly well traveled and not a particularly likely place to dump a body. Nevertheless, that was the indelible impression that was left on her mind.

Judy tried to shake the vision, but when it simply wouldn't go away, she decided to go down to the local police department. Once there, she drove around the block a few times, wondering what she could say that wouldn't make her look foolish. At last she went inside and asked to speak to a detective. Even then, the officer had to coax the information out of her. Reluctantly, she told him about her dream, the vivid nature of the images, and the fact that she just couldn't shake it. Intrigued, the detective took her back to a large map of the area that showed all of the canyons in the surrounding area. Without hesitation Judy zeroed in on an area to the north and east. It was a smaller canyon with only one two-lane secondary road running through it. Judy had no idea why she was drawn to that spot, but then she had no idea why she was going through all of this to begin with.

They returned to the detective's office, and he was suddenly very serious. The police, he told her, had found a truck in that general area that had been torched. It belonged to a nurse who had been missing for several days. Until Judy walked in the door, the police had absolutely nothing to go on. For all they knew, the woman could have run off with the love of her life, and vandals could have torched the truck.

"No," Judy told them, "she was murdered, and her body is still up there in that canyon."

The police agreed to launch a search and told her to go home, but aside from the one detective to whom she had spoken personally, Judy got the distinct feeling that they really didn't have their heart in it. Judy decided that she wouldn't leave it up to them.

She did go home, but still haunted by the persistent images, she gathered up her children and headed for the canyon she had identified on the map. Maybe she would recognize something, some piece of terrain that she had seen in the dream, and at least narrow the search area. When she reached the top of the canyon, she stopped and got out of the car. There was an eerie silence, and she was suddenly overtaken by feelings of anxiety. She was about to get back in the car when she noticed tire tracks. She knelt down and touched them with the tips of her fingers. Immediately the feelings of anxiety increased dramatically. This was where it had happened, she was certain, and her only desire now was to get out of there as quickly as possible.

Judy got back in the car and was hurrying down the mountain when her daughter called out.

"Stop! Back there," her daughter said excitedly, "I saw something white."

Judy backed up and stopped the car. She and her daughter got out and made their way toward the spot where the girl thought she had seen something. As it turned out, what she had seen were the white shoes the nurse was wearing. They had found the body.

"Hurry," Judy said, turning her daughter away from the

gruesome sight, "we have to tell the police."

Judy hurried back to the car. They were heading down the canyon once more when they spotted a police officer. They hailed him down, told him what they had found, and described the location of the body. The officer told them there was nothing more that they could do and instructed them to go home. At last, it was over with—or so she thought.

Charged with Murder

The police recovered the body, and later that evening, two police officers came to Judy's door. They asked her to come down to the station with them. Judy quickly agreed, but when they got there, she was asked to take a polygraph test. Again she agreed without hesitation. A short time later, Judy was arrested and charged with the crime.

For the next three days, Judy was behind bars, loudly protesting her innocence. Then police got a tip and picked up three men in a neighboring county who confessed to the murder.

The prosecuting attorney was unrepentant. "She knew details of the crime that only the killer should have known," he said. "My hypothesis is, she picked up the information about the abduction on the local grapevine and fabricated the story."

The prosecutor's attitude tells us a great deal about the level of acceptance most officials have toward psychic phenomena. Faced with the reality that Judy did not commit the crime, and admitting that she knew things about it that only the killer would know, he still insisted that he did the right thing by throwing her in jail. The more obvious fact— that she could not possibly have picked up things from the local grapevine that *only the killer would know*—seemed to have completely eluded him.

For her part, Judy is a true accidental psychic. She says

that she never had any kind of psychic experience before—nor in the two decades since. She hopes that she never has one again. She did, however, sue the county for wrongful arrest and incarceration.

It would be unfair to suggest that practicing psychics who volunteer their time and talents to help police solve crimes frequently wind up being arrested. In fact, the case we have just described is the only one we know of where the psychic was actually put in jail solely on the basis of the information given to the police. In most cases, the psychic is simply given a wide berth by those not directly involved with the investigation. It is also true that psychic detectives do not solve every case in which they're asked to participate. Indeed, the ledger may fall on the debit side when all the cases are added up. But that's hardly the point.

Consider the circumstances under which the psychic is asked to work. In almost every case, the police have come to a dead end. Some cases have lain dormant for years. Usually, the psychic is provided with only the barest details with which to work. And given the nature of psychic awareness, more often than not, the psychic isn't even sure what the impressions mean. Given all this, it's a wonder that psychics have any success at all.

America's Best-Known Psychic Detective

Most psychics are fully aware of the drawbacks but continue to offer their services anyway, no matter how remote their chance of success. Dorothy Allison is one such psychic detective. She has been featured on television shows such as A&E's "Unexplained" and "Sightings" and NBC's "Dateline." She will go just about anywhere her help is requested and adamantly refuses to accept any money for her services. According to "Sightings," she has a remarkable record of achievement.

In one of her more bizarre cases, Dorothy was called by a detective and asked to come to Canada. A young girl had been missing for some time, and by the time she was called in, the police had run out of options. There were no leads and no clues. In a telephone conversation with the detective, Dorothy said that she was experiencing some kind of "psychic interference." But she agreed to come up and do what she could anyway.

Strangely, the psychic could get nothing on the girl the detective was concerned about. But she insisted that there was someone else—another girl—and something terrible had happened to her. Driving past a lake near the town where the girl had disappeared, Dorothy began to experience the same kind of psychic interference that she had during the phone call. A girl's body was in that lake, she told police, and her leg would be the first thing to be found.

A few days later, fishermen made a grim discovery. They pulled up a cement block with a girl's leg protruding from it. An immediate search was undertaken. In all, eight cement blocks were retrieved, each containing a body part of a young girl.

The detective felt certain that they had found his missing victim, but the coroner's report identified the girl in the cement blocks as another missing teenager whose disappearance had only been reported a few days earlier. The physical characteristics of the two missing girls were strikingly similar: Both were about the same height and weight, both had naturally brown hair dyed blond, and both wore braces.

Back home in the United States, a year passed before Dorothy Allison would be contacted by the detective again. He still hadn't been able to locate the original missing girl, and the psychic still could not offer him any help. But another victim *would* be found, she told him, and within a week. Dorothy gave the detective an amazingly detailed description, even though he assured her that no such person had been reported missing.

The girl would be found covered with brush, she told him. She told the detective that he would hear trickling water nearby and see a white fence. Within a week, a young girl with long dark hair was indeed reported missing. She was found a few days later, her body hurriedly buried under some brush. A nearby culvert provided the sound of trickling water, and across the road was a white rail fence.

Unfortunately, Dorothy Allison could not give the detective a description of the murderer. One more murder would occur before a young woman would come forward and confess that it was she and her husband who had committed all the murders, thus bringing to a close one of the most bizarre crime sprees in Canadian history. Although Dorothy Allison had not been able to help solve the case, the accuracy of her descriptions of the victims, *well before* their bodies were discovered, left a lasting impression on the detective.

If Peter Hurkos is the world's best-known psychic detective, it's fair to say that Dorothy Allison holds that distinction in America. Her most recent case was made public by "Sightings" in January 1998. Allison was called in to help solve the case of a grandmother who was raped and murdered in a small town in Alabama. The sheriff had never worked with a psychic before, but was impressed with his first meeting. Having only the victim's birthdate and the date of the murder to work with, she correctly identified where the crime had taken place and how the murder was committed. But there is something decidedly different in this instance. Working with a retired New York police sketch artist, Dorothy Allison has given the police, and through "Sightings" the world, a picture of what the murderer looks like. It will be interesting to see if Dorothy Allison proves to be right once again.

Gerard Croiset Jr.

Like psychic healers, some psychic detectives apparently can receive their images over great distances. Gerard Croiset Jr., the son of a world famous Dutch psychic, demonstrated this ability by assisting in the case of two missing girls thousands of miles away in South Carolina. The two girls had gone for a walk along the beach near their home and were never seen again. One girl's mother, desperate to find her daughter, heard about Croiset and wrote him a letter pleading for his help.

Within a matter of days, the mother received Croiset's response. In it he drew a sketch of the beach, which he had never seen, including such details as a bus stop and a parked bulldozer, along with a page and a half of comments. "The girls," he said, will be there [on the beach] together." The police found the girls where Croiset said they would be, and they were together. They had been murdered and buried, side by side, in shallow graves in the sand.

Psychic Healers Help People Get Well

Jane Katra

Jane Katra holds a doctorate in public health education and has been a psychic healer for more than twenty years. She is the coauthor of *Miracles of Mind: Exploring Nonlocal Consciousness and Spiritual Healing*. In 1974, Katra went to the Philippines to investigate psychic surgeons. In the following viewpoint, she admits that while some psychic healers are charlatans, others genuinely help people get well. She believes it should not matter if the healers are frauds if their patients get well due to their faith in the healer or with prayer. During her time in the Philippines, Katra had a dream in which she received power to heal people through therapeutic touch. She asserts that there is a strong mind-to-mind connection in psychic healing. Katra also maintains that there is a transfer of energy between the healer and the patient that helps the patient get well.

Excerpted from *Miracles of Mind: Exploring Nonlocal Consciousness and Spiritual Healing*, by Russell Targ and Jane Katra (Novato, CA: New World Library, 1998). Copyright © 1998 by Russell Targ and Jane Katra. Reprinted with permission.

The reason I had gone to the Philippines in the first place was to investigate firsthand what was going on with the Philippine healers, or the so-called psychic surgeons. I was on the last leg of a yearlong trek around Southeast Asia, and I was ready to return home. But I had promised myself that I would see "the healers" before going back to Seattle. A friend who had multiple sclerosis had gone to see the healers in the Philippines the year before. She had not been cured, but she was not at all sorry that she had spent so much money to go there and visit them. She felt her symptoms had gone into remission after her trip. She also told me that everyone in her travel group felt improved, too. She said that she knew that some healers used sleight of hand to make it look like they were pulling tumors out of people's insides, but that one woman in her group had apparently been completely healed of cancer. My friend said that something remarkable and unusual was going on in the Philippines. She suggested I check it out for myself, and see what I could make of it. . . .

Watching a Surgery

After I had learned where the healers worked in Manila, I tried to figure out how to watch them do whatever it was that they did. I contemplated the problem, as I wandered around the crowded second floor of the Manila Hotel, where several Americans had come to be healed. Before I had time to meet anyone, a bright-eyed, salt-and-pepper-haired man came right up to me and introduced himself. With a sense of urgency, he explained that he was next in line to see the healer Thelma Zuniga. Then he anxiously asked if I would be willing to video his hemorrhoid operation.

I was taken off guard, and before I had time to answer, he handed me his camera, and showed me where to look and what to push. "Now, don't be bashful!" he urged. "Get right up close to her hands, and get it all on film! This is amazing stuff! I brought my seventy-two-year-old mother here last year, and they took out her tumors and healed her cancer. So this year, I came to have my hemorrhoids out, and I want to show my friends and family what they did when I go home!" So I said, "Okay." I had only the vaguest notion of what a hemorrhoid was, but the situation provided me with a perfect vantage point from which to carry out my mission.

I got right up close and filmed the healer, Thelma, pressing on his bare buttocks with her fingers. Watery, bloodlike fluid oozed down his thighs, and in a minute or so some purplish tissue appeared in Thelma's fingers. It looked like clusters of tiny grapes. She wiped his bottom with a wad of cotton and said, "Okay. Finished." As he pulled up his boxers, I looked askance and mumbled something, handed him his camera, and made a hasty getaway.

The next morning when I returned to the second-floor lobby of the hotel, I reluctantly encountered the man again. I asked him, sheepishly, "So, how are your hemorrhoids today?" and he said, "Honey, they're gone! It's great!" I questioned him skeptically, "Are you sure?" He exclaimed, "You bet I'm sure! I've been tucking those darn things in every morning for the past fifteen years, and when I tell you they're gone, believe me, I know what I'm talking about! They're gone!"

That day, another unexpected event took place. Thelma invited me into the hotel room where she was doing her operations. Her assistant told her that I was a reporter, and that I shouldn't be allowed to observe, but Thelma shushed her away, and turned toward the buxom Swiss woman who was disrobing for a varicose vein operation. The woman lay facedown on the bed, clad only in her underwear, and Thelma began to massage her thighs laboriously, as red fluid squished and splattered all around us.

Thelma told the woman and her concerned husband to pray. The husband stood at his wife's side with his head bowed, and he held her hand as they murmured hushed words together in German. I was moved by their devotion to each other and to their God, by the man's gentle sensitivity to his wife, and by his relinquishing of control to Thelma. They had something I had rarely seen before, something that was entirely foreign to me. These seemingly intelligent people believed in a Higher Power that was real and had meaning for them, and they believed that their prayers might be beneficial for healing. For me, it was like watching a play. I could not understand why they would spend their money to come here and pray in a hotel room, while this Philippine woman put on a spectacular performance of trickery with animal entrails and blood. It was as if we were all agreeing to participate in some cathartic ritual.

All of a sudden, I realized that I was *in* the play, but no one had ever given me a script. I was enveloped in the loving, prayerful ambiance in that hotel room. All was quiet for a few moments as I felt my mind joined with theirs, hoping for healing. . . .

Sick People Feeling Better

After a week, I'd seen many so-called psychic surgeries, most of which my rational mind told me were sleight of hand, and yet which my observations told me were efficacious to varying degrees. I saw things that looked like animal entrails appearing as if they were being pulled out of people, and things that looked like real incisions cut into people, through which globs of who-knows-what appeared. I mostly saw sick people feeling better, speaking a common language of hope and fellowship to each other, in a community of affirmative expectation.

I was looking forward to seeing the renowned healer, Alex Orbito, do his famous eye-check procedure. I decided to team up with an American woman who was writing for a Yakima, Washington, newspaper. With two pairs of eyes to scrutinize, I thought we ought to be able to discern what was going on. We walked over to the chapel courtyard where Orbito was doing his procedures. Long lines of Filipino people of all ages were waiting patiently to be treated.

The reporter stood on one side of the patient's head and watched Orbito's hands, while I stood on the other side with my face down, eye-to-eye with the patient. It looked as if Alex had his finger behind the man's eyeball, and that the eyeball was popped forward in its socket and pushed off to one side. I thought to myself, it might be easy to palm a fake eyeball, but why can't I see the man's real eye in there? And how does he get the glass eye to just hang there? I asked the patient, "Doesn't that hurt?" and he answered, "No, but it feels strange—a bit ticklish. I can feel his finger in the socket."

Later I wished I had asked him if he could see with his dangling eye. I'm not sure what the procedure was meant to accomplish, or whether it was helpful or not, but it certainly was impressive to watch. When I compared notes with the other reporter after Orbito's eye show, we were each disappointed that the other didn't have an intelligent explanation for what we saw.

At that point, I had seen many surgeries. I didn't know what to believe, and I didn't trust what I thought I saw. Some of the operations I observed had been quite bloody, and others not at all. When I asked Thelma why that was, she told me that "Some people do better with lots of blood." I assumed she had meant that they more strongly believed in the power of God to heal them, or that they healed themselves better.

Why did the healers palm chicken guts if they could re-arrange eyeballs painlessly, and remove hemorrhoids with their bare fingers? I thought I had seen a tiny razor blade under one healer's fingernail, so, aha! He wasn't cutting people open with his finger! He was simply using a razor blade! (And then reaching inside people's bodies with his bare hands and pulling out tumors, while the people felt no pain?) Or did he cut people and use chicken guts, so they would believe they were being operated on—and actually heal themselves?

I gave up the idea of writing anything about the healers for the newspaper. It wasn't possible for me to figure out what was actually going on. Smarter people than I had been perplexed by this. It didn't seem to be all fraud, all the time. And besides, I wanted people to get better, so why did it matter *how* it happened?

So what if the so-called operations were frauds, as long as people got well? If reporters think it's a problem, but sick people don't, is it meaningful to ask if the psychic surgeries are real or fake? Maybe, as the Buddhist philosopher Na-garjuna postulated, they are both real and not real.[1]

In any case, when I tried to make sense of it, my headache began. It was made worse by the fact that I had barely eaten anything in the past few days, because I was out of money and was waiting for the arrival of funds via Western Union. Also, I had not been sleeping well at all. In retrospect, my stress, my unintended fast and dehydration, physical ex-haustion from months on the road, and the assaults by the healers on my view of reality all contributed to a situation that, in many ways, resembles a contemporary shamanic vi-sion quest, or brainwashing.

I once heard it said that "mystical experiences are to religion what basic research is to science."

—Anne Gordon
A Book of Saints

I have no recollection of even one more moment of pain after I prayed. In fact, I have no recollection of being awake at all after praying that night. What I do remember is the most vivid, startling, phenomenal dream I have ever had in my life. It disturbed me so much that I thought I was going crazy. . . .

The dream I had after praying gave me instructions about how I myself would do healing with my own hands. This information came to me from an extremely bright light that communicated with me in a dream that I did not want, and patiently debated with me when I declined to believe or accept the instructions. The voice in the light conveyed compassion when I began to sob out of fear that I was cracking up. The dream greatly frightened me, because when I tried to escape the instructions and the light by waking up, I was unable to awaken myself. . . .

In that long-ago dream, I was told that *the very next day*, I would put my hands on a stranger, and she would be healed. I vehemently denied it. "No way! Absolutely not! I wouldn't do that to a friend, much less to a stranger!" The voice told me that it would, indeed, happen, but that I would not remember my dream or these instructions until after the healing had occurred, because I was so distraught.

I argued with the light-being. "I won't do it! Even if you say I will be able to do healing, I won't! You can't make me do it!" The being was amused. "No one will force you. You will do it on your own accord." "Please give me some sign," I asked, "Show me, somehow, that I have not lost my mind. Please!"

The voice in my dream told me that in due time I would meet two men who would help me to understand. I was told that each man would approach me and introduce himself. As I wondered to myself how I would know the difference between a man coming to offer guidance, and one whose motives were not so pure, my concern was addressed. I was told specific words that the mentors would use during the encounters, so that I would be able to identify them as the people who would be trustworthy and helpful.

Then the voice in the light told me to hold out my hand. So I did. "Stretch out your arm," it communicated, so I did that. Then a most amazing thing happened.

I was zapped with blinding light. I felt a sensation much like one I experienced when I was four, when I stuck some wires into an electrical outlet. A powerful surge of electrifying current passed down my arm, and coursed through my entire body, with a *whoosh*. An explosion of light erupted within me. Fireworks went off inside my head. I was stunned, and overcome by the brightness. I felt like I had no body. I was radiating light. I was pure energy. I was elation.

I awoke to find myself standing in the middle of the room. I knew it was no longer night by the light coming through the windows. My right arm was outstretched above me. My nightgown was sopping, and clung to my wet body as tears rolled down my face. I felt absolutely energized. Completely alert. Blissfully radiant. Ecstatic. Not at all like a person who had been tormented by unrelenting pain for days. Not at all like someone who hadn't been sleeping well, or hadn't eaten anything in recent memory. All the pain I'd felt the previous night was gone. . . .

My First Healing

As I rode the elevator to the second floor of the Manila Hotel, I thought how unusual it was to feel so well-rested and vitalized in my physical body, while my mind was obviously so confused. I felt like a different person from the one who had been suffering with the headache . . . whenever that was. It seemed so long ago.

The elevator doors opened, and I stepped out into a small sitting area. As I headed towards Thelma's room, I noticed a woman lying on a couch, off to one side of the hallway. As I approached her, I saw that she was agitated. As I came closer, I heard her groan, and I sensed that she was not well. I asked, "Are you all right?" And she said, "No," that she had been having a horrible migraine headache for two days, that she was nauseated and dizzy and couldn't walk, and that she was in agony. Her husband had gone to look for a doctor.

I asked her if she would like me to wait with her, and she said, "Yes." As I stood there, watching her suffer, I asked her, "Would you like me to massage your scalp while we wait? Maybe it would help." And she said, "Sure. Try anything."

As I bent over her, with my hands over her hair, I tried to decide what to do. Just as I was about to put my fingers on her head, I got the idea that it might be better if I massaged the back of her neck. But she was lying on her back, and I couldn't get to her neck without asking her to change her position. So I decided to go back to my original plan, and massage her scalp. Just as I was deciding whether to start above her ears, or below them, she heaved a huge sigh of relief, and exclaimed, "Oh! *Thank* you! Oh, what a relief! Thank you so much."

I was totally taken aback. "But I haven't done anything yet! I was just about to start!" She quickly exclaimed, "Oh, yes, you did! I felt it when you brought your hands near. I felt the surge of energy! It felt so wonderful! It took the pain right away! My head felt so light. It was such a relief! It felt like your hands opened a dam, and all the pain just poured out! Thank you so much!"

Then I remembered my dream from the night before. It

all came back to me. And I shook my head in disbelief at what I'd done, and thought to myself, "You were right. I did do it! . . . And she was a total stranger!" I looked at my hands and wondered why I hadn't felt any energy leaving them, if the woman had felt energy flowing into her. If I had done something, wouldn't I know it? How could something like that happen, with my body, without my knowledge? Who was doing this? What was going on? I was more bewildered than ever.

I am now aware that laboratory data offers strong evidence for the existence of a mind-to-mind connection in psychic healing. Among people who actively practice healing today, however, the mind-to-mind hypothesis would be a minority opinion. Millions of Asians, Indians, Egyptians, and Polynesians throughout history have believed in an "exchange of energy" associated with psychic healing. Their experiences are not unlike those of modern day practitioners of Therapeutic Touch, Reiki, Polarity, Joh Rei, Huna, Raimondi, Chi Gong, or Pranic Healing, who also feel that energy is transmitted between healers and their patients.

Note

1. Richard P. Hayes, "Nagarjuna's Appeal," *Journal of Indian Philosophy*, 1994, pp. 299–378.

A Remote Viewing Experiment Was Successful

Dale E. Graff

Dale E. Graff is the founder and director of Project Stargate, the U.S. government's program that investigated and used remote viewing as a means of espionage. In the following viewpoint, Graff describes the first time he participated and oversaw a remote viewing experiment. The remote viewer in New York City accurately described the caves Graff and his two companions toured in Ohio. Graff maintains that while the success of this experiment does not prove the existence of remote viewing, it shows that its potential should not be ignored.

A new or unusual experience usually remains vivid in memory throughout our lives. I'm sure we can all recall the

Excerpted from *Tracks in the Psychic Wilderness: An Exploration of Remote Viewing, ESP, Precognitive Dreaming, and Synchronicity,* by Dale E. Graff (Boston: Element, 1998). Copyright © 1998 by Element Books, Inc. Reprinted by permission of the author. Website: http://www.chesapeake.net/~baygraff/ E-mail: baygraff@chesapeake.net.

essence, even details, of that first day in school, first date, or first presentation. Both positive and negative events, when charged with strong emotion or special significance, are never far from the surface of our consciousness. Certain startling experiences, especially those that run contrary to our notion of reality, have a similar effect. My first encounter with remote viewing phenomenon left just such a lasting impression with me. I occasionally review that experience, reliving its impact. Although I was only an observer, the event was a turning point in my life. It motivated me to move deeper into an inner voyage of discovery.

My professional career of aerospace engineering and physics left little room for the subjective, though I was certainly aware of creativity, intuitive flashes, and occasional unusual coincidences. At that time I believed there was some purely rational basis for these "soft experiences." The laws of chance, it seemed, could account for all coincidences. Some of my childhood experiences were puzzling and suggested a psi origin. However, I eventually accepted a conventional view of reality and disregarded them.

The Remote Viewer

In 1976, when I became contract manager for remote viewing research, one of my first actions was to set up and observe a viewing experiment. The principal researchers at SRI [Stanford Research Institute], Dr. Harold Puthoff and Russell Targ, visited Dayton and put me in phone contact with Hella Hammid, a project remote viewer, while she was visiting in New York City. Hella lived in Los Angeles and was a professional photographer.

Calling her from Dayton, I introduced myself as a colleague of Hal's and invited her to participate in a remote viewing experiment later that day. She was eager to see what she could do. All she knew was that we could be anywhere in the U.S. We had never met and she did not know where I lived or worked.

Earlier that day I had prepared a list of ten diverse places in the Dayton area that would be good potential remote viewing targets. They included sites on Wright Patterson Air Force Base as well as locations around the city. I intended to select one of them at random shortly before Hal, Russ, and I went there as beacon persons. I made sure that Hal and Russ did not know what targets were on my list. I didn't want to risk possible criticism that they might have inadvertently given clues of my target possibilities to Hella. If Hella succeeded, a critic might claim her success was due to a good guess rather than remote viewing.

Although Hella sounded very enthusiastic, friendly, and cooperative, I felt somewhat uncomfortable. I could only hope my feelings of doubt would not affect the experiment. Much depended on this event, even though it could only serve as a demonstration of remote viewing—not as proof—should the results turn out to be successful. Likewise, a failure would not negate remote viewing. I needed to be reasonably convinced that something of potential use could result from this research. Otherwise I might not get the project off to a good start. I had many pressing demands on my time and I suspected that working on a topic as way-out as remote viewing would give me plenty of headaches.

Since I was not experienced at selecting targets, I began to have doubts about how I had constructed that target pool. As I reviewed them, I realized many sites had similar features, differing only in scale or size. The Air Force Logistics Command building, though larger, resembles the Air Force Institute of Technology Headquarters, which I had on my list. The old Dayton Post Office has large steps and columns similar to those at the Xenia Courthouse, though not as

Waltham High School
Library/Media Cente

many. Others were too complex and would be too busy and confusing to Hella, or they could fit most anything she described. For a simple demonstration, these technical problems may not have mattered, but I needed to observe something more convincing than how well a few of Hella's sketches might match assorted buildings or structures in the Dayton area. I wanted to observe an unambiguous, successful remote viewing experiment.

As I pondered this dilemma, an idea hit me: Why not select a truly unique target? And if it were some distance from Dayton, then it couldn't be argued that Hella might have known where Hal was visiting and had simply made a good guess. It was a good idea, but what could be such a target?

Ohio Caverns

Pacing around, a great target occurred to me. Very unique and very isolated, it was thirty-five miles away, near Columbus, Ohio. I rounded up Hal and Russ and proceeded to drive out of Dayton. They were curious about the location of my target, since they suspected I had selected a site somewhere on base. I drove on silently, keeping the destination to myself. They were quite surprised when I pulled into the parking lot of the Ohio Caverns.

"This is a great target!" exclaimed Hal, "We have never attempted a cave or anything underground. Hella ought to enjoy this."

I was pleased to hear such confidence. I still had many doubts.

Taking in the scenery on the cavern grounds, Russ pointed out another advantage to using this site as the target. It would give us an opportunity to observe how a remote viewer would do when describing someone who is underground, where low-frequency waves are highly attenuated. Some theorists, including Soviet ESP researcher I.M. Kogan, had proposed that low-frequency brain waves have a role in psi.

We daydreamed about doing a remote viewing experiment from a submarine, since seawater blocks out most electromagnetic radiation. Remote viewing success with a submarine deep in the ocean would rule out electromagnetics as a carrier of psi information. (Later in the program, fortuitous circumstances would permit us to carry out just such an experiment.)

We had coffee, then joined a tour shortly before the time Hella would begin her remote viewing six hundred miles away. Slowly we strolled through archways of overhanging vines, entered through a narrow doorway, and descended into the darkness of Ohio's largest cavern, formed eons ago by water dissolving limestone under the rolling hillsides of central Ohio. We were surrounded by tall white and beige stalagmites jutting up from the ground; similar-looking stalactites loomed down from the dark ceiling. They reflected a golden glow from hundreds of bare bulbs stretching along the passageways.

We moved slowly through the cave, chilled by the cold, misty air, inching across slippery paths, squeezing through a maze of rocky tunnels, and crossing shaky bridges that spanned crystal clear pools. Water dripped from the high ceiling. Occasionally, the tour guide called for silence and turned off the lights. In this dark, eerie vault, it was easy to feel primeval connections to the earth's chaotic origin, to the steady flow of time and evolution.

I could not help feeling a deep sense of awe, of mystery. Occasionally, my musings drifted toward Hella. I wondered if she had linked up with us, and how she might be experiencing, or interpreting, our adventure into this fascinating deep cave. There was no question: She would either be right on or way off. This experiment would either be a hit or a miss.

After forty-five minutes, we came to the cave exit. Steep metal stairs angled toward the faint light of the outside world 150 feet above. A loud, metallic booming echoed as we stomped upward. We filed through a heavy metal door and emerged into a bright, sunny afternoon, shielding and blinking our eyes. The tour guide heaved the massive door shut.

At the agreed-upon time, I placed a call to Hella. My anxiety grew to an almost intolerable level as the phone rang and rang. Finally she answered.

"We are through visiting the site, Hella. What did you see?" I asked.

Her Vision

Our protocol was just to listen to Hella and give no feedback until after we had received her written material. I waited anxiously for her reply.

"This is strange. . . . I don't know what you guys got yourselves into. It sure is scary! I saw . . . a maze of caves . . . brightly lit. You were in a misty place . . . deep underground."

I remained quiet, motionless, hardly believing what I was hearing. How could she sense our site so well? There was no doubt; she had sensed the exact nature of the Ohio Caverns. She continued describing her impressions.

"At first I saw something like a wine cellar entrance, and an archway with wisteria, leading to an underground world. Then I saw caves, or mines . . . deep shafts . . . an earthy smell . . . moist passages. Silent, not much sound . . . scary . . . a golden glow all over. Only a few people. A very special place."

She paused briefly, as though reliving her experience, then continued: "There is something humming, throbbing. . . . You come to . . . a steel wall."

She remained quiet, no doubt anxious about how she had done. I thanked her, being careful not to show a reaction, and told her she would know the target as soon as we received her written scripts. I hung up and slowly turned to Hal and Russ, shaking my head.

"She got it! She got the target! I can't believe this. She was right on!"

Hal and Russ were elated. They knew it was important for me to see remote viewing first hand. I drove back to Dayton slowly. We talked continuously about the experiment, seeing it as a benchmark. For me, it certainly was significant. With a few brief, excitement-filled words, Hella had brought me directly into the world of remote viewing. I could sense her enthusiasm and courage. My solid view of reality had to bend a little. I now had to make room for a deeper level of awareness I had suppressed and ignored.

Hal, Russ, and I talked of the many challenges ahead, and how to best apply remote viewing. Could we find a way to improve accuracy? Could remote viewers do better in identifying or interpreting their perceptions? We had a lot to think about.

Back in Dayton, I turned to Hal and said: "Why don't we credit this experiment to Hella by naming it 'Hella's Cave'?"

"I think she'll be pleased," he said.

"And she didn't have to pay for the tour," I quipped.

We received Hella's written scripts several days later. After her remote viewing session, she had attempted to interpret her impressions. She thought our "scary place" was something "far out," possibly an entrance to an "underground city" or something "nuclear." It is not uncommon for remote viewers to miss the analytical aspects of the target. Specific names, numbers, and functions are difficult for remote viewers to detect and are not nearly as reliable as drawings or sketches. Even though she missed the function of our recreational site, she had most everything else correct.

While positive proof could not be derived from just one experiment, Hella's Cave gave me an unforgettable reference point. I now found the confidence I needed to continue with my emerging remote viewing activity. Feeling a new dedication, I knew I could give this effort whatever professional energy it demanded. Now I was willing to square off with the critics.

I had taken Hal and Russ into that cave to explore the boundaries of remote viewing, but that misty cave also brought me closer to unknown dimensions deep within myself. Hella's Cave was my initiation into remote viewing and helped begin an exciting adventure—a voyage of inner discovery.

Chapter 2

Fact or Fiction?

Evidence Against Psychic Abilities

Psychic Powers Are Against the Laws of Nature

Robert Todd Carroll

Robert Todd Carroll is the editor of *The Skeptics Dictionary*, an online book that provides definitions, arguments, and essays on the supernatural, occult, paranormal, and pseudo-scientific subjects. In the following viewpoint, he argues that no one has been able to scientifically prove that he or she has psychic powers despite several long-standing offers of substantial monetary rewards. According to Carroll, psychics live by the same laws of nature as everyone else; therefore, their claims of being able to communicate with the dead contradict natural law. He asserts that most psychics who perform a reading are able to deceive their clients by making educated guesses based on conscious and unconscious clues from their marks. He believes the world would be very different if psychic power truly existed. Carroll concludes that people who claim to be psychic are most likely frauds who

From "Psychic," by Robert Todd Carroll, *The Skeptics Dictionary: A Guide to the New Millennium*, www.skepdic.com, July 27, 2001. Copyright © 2001 by Robert Todd Carroll. Reprinted with permission.

take advantage of people's gullibility or are deluded into deceiving themselves that they have psychic powers.

"When confidential information leaks out of an organization, people suspect a spy, not a psychic."
—John Allen Paulos, *Innumeracy*

As an adjective, *psychic* refers to forces or agencies of a paranormal nature. As a noun, *psychic* refers to a medium or a person who has paranormal powers.

James Randi, who has tested many people who think they have psychic abilities, has found that when he has tested the alleged paranormal powers of psychics (1) they had never before tested their powers under controlled conditions, and (2) those who don't offer preposterous rationalizations for their inability to perform seem genuinely baffled at their failure. Often, psychics are not frauds; they genuinely believe in their powers. But they've never tested their powers in any meaningful way. Randi offers $1,000,000 to anyone who can demonstrate psychic powers. The Australian Skeptics will throw in an additional $100,000 (Australian) for the psychic and $20,000 for anyone "who nominates a person who successfully completes the Australian Skeptics Challenge." B. Premanand of the Indian Skeptic will throw in another 100,000 rupees.

To believe in the ability of a person to channel spirits, to "hear" or "feel" the voices or presence of the dead, to "see" the past, the future or what is presently in another's mind, to make contact with a realm of reality that transcends natural laws is to believe in something highly improbable. Psychics don't rely on psychics to warn them of impending disasters. Psychics don't predict their own deaths or diseases. They go to the dentist like the rest of us. They're as surprised and disturbed as the rest of us when they have to call a plumber or an electrician to fix some defect at home. Their planes are delayed without their being able to anticipate the delays. If they want to know something about Abraham Lincoln, they go to the library; they don't try to talk to Abe's spirit. In short, psychics live by the known laws of nature except when they are playing the psychic game with people. Psychics aren't overly worried about other psychics reading their minds and revealing their innermost secrets to the world. No casino has ever banned psychics from the gaming room because there is no need.

The improbability of there being a paranormal realm is argued for in many entries in the *Skeptic's Dictionary*. If it is improbable that the paranormal is real, then it is improbable that psychics are tapping into the paranormal realm. Why then are psychics so popular with young and old, stupid and intelligent, ignorant and wise alike?

The main reasons for belief in such paranormal powers as clairvoyance and clairaudience are (1) the perceived accuracy of psychic predictions and readings; (2) the seemingly uncanny premonitions which many people have, especially in dreams; and (3) the seemingly fantastic odds against such premonitions or predictions being correct by coincidence or chance.

However, the accuracy of psychic predictions is grossly overrated. The belief in the accuracy of clairvoyants such as Edgar Cayce and Jeanne Dixon is due to several factors, including mass media error and hype. For example, it has been repeatedly reported in the mass media that Jeanne Dixon predicted the assassination of President Kennedy. She did not. The *New York Times* helped spread the myth that Edgar Cayce transformed from an illiterate into a healer when hypnotized. One of the more egregious cases of mass media complicity in promoting belief in psychics is the case of "psychic" Tamara Rand, producer Dick Maurice, and talk show host Gary Grecco of KNTV in Las Vegas. All conspired to deceive the public by claiming that a video tape of a "Dick Maurice Show," on which Rand predicts the assassination attempt by John Hinkley on Ronald Reagan, was done on January 6, 1981. The tape was actually made on March 31, 1991, a day after Hinkley shot Reagan (Steiner).

Another reason the accuracy of psychic predictions is grossly overrated is because many people do not understand how psychics use techniques such as warm and cold reading. Also, many people lack an understanding of confirmation bias and The Law of Truly Large Numbers. The accuracy of premonitions and prophecies is also grossly exaggerated because of lack of understanding of confirmation bias and The Law of Truly Large Numbers; their accuracy is also exaggerated because of ignorance about how memory works, especially about how dreams and premonitions are often filled in after the fact.

The strongest kind of evidence for psychic power comes from witnessing an alleged psychic perform. Some performers seem to be able to do things that require paranormal powers; these are the masters of the art of conjuring. Others seem to be able to tell us things about ourselves and our departed loved ones that only we should know; these are the masters of cold reading. Others surreptitiously gather information about us and deceive us into thinking they obtained their data by psychic means.

The success of numerous hoaxes by fraudulent psychics testifies to the difficulty of seeing through the performance. Psychologist Ray Hyman, who worked as a "psychic" to help pay his way through college, claims that the most common method used by psychics is "cold reading" and offers the following Guide to Cold Reading:

1. You must act with confidence. You don't need to be ar-

rogant. In fact, you will probably benefit by pretending to be humble. James van Praagh and John Edward repeatedly warn their marks that they aren't always accurate, that they don't know how their power works, that they misinterpret things, etc. But they never give any sign that they are not really communicating with the dead.

2. You must do your research. You have to be up on the latest statistics (e.g., most plane crashes are in April; most planes have something red on their tails). You have to know what people in general are like from polls and surveys. Also, you must pick up in casual conversation before a performance any information that might be useful later, like talking to a cameraman in the afternoon and then during the evening performance you are "contacted" by his dead father, whom he told you all about that afternoon.

3. You must convince the mark that he or she will be the reason for success or failure. This is actually true because it is the mark who will provide all the vital information that seems so shocking and revealing. It is human nature to find meaning, so this is not a difficult chore. The mark will bring significance to much of what you throw at him or her. If you bring up "June" and get no response, you make the mark feel like they're not remembering properly. If you say "8, the 8th month, 8-years, August" and somebody bites by saying "Dad died in August" and the mark thinks it was *you* who told *her* that fact rather than the other way around. When you say "I see a watch, a bracelet, something on the wrist" and the mark says "I put my necklace in mom's casket." You say "Right. She thanks you for it, too." Everybody thinks you knew she put a necklace in the casket and they will forget that you were fishing for some jewelry on the wrist.

4. Be observant. Does the person have expensive jewelry on but worn out clothes? Is she wearing a pin with the letter 'K' on it. (You better know that 'Kevin' is a good guess

here. But it doesn't matter, really. Since, when the mark tells you the name of the person, she'll think you are the one who told her the name!)

5. Use flattery and pretend you know more than you do.

The list goes on, but you get the idea. What looks like psychic power is little more than a game of twenty-questions, or a fishing expedition, with *the mark providing all the relevant details and connecting all the dots*, while the "psychic" appears to be getting messages from beyond. Of course, sometimes the "psychic" is simply an observant, thoughtful person, who says things appropriate for the age and gender of the subject. For example, one of my students—right out of high school, tall, handsome, strong and athletic—was told by a "psychic" to stay away from the opposite sex or he'd be having a baby. The student became an immediate convert. He'd already gotten a girl pregnant and had a daughter. Good advice became proof of psychic power in this young man's mind. She also told him other things "nobody could have known," such as that he had once thrown up all over himself and crapped in his pants. He apparently had done this as a young man and didn't realize that she was describing a nearly universal situation for babies.

The deception can be more dramatic than cold reading, of course. According to Lamar Keene, a "reformed psychic," some people seek psychic advice from professional psychics who exchange information on their marks. Some psychics do what is called a "warm reading," i.e., they have done research on you and that's why they know things they shouldn't know. Still others are magicians who try to pass off their conjuring skills as paranormal powers.

If Psychic Power Existed . . .

It has also been argued that if psychic power existed, to use it would be "a gross and unethical violation of privacy" and "professions that involve deception would be worthless" (Radford). There wouldn't be any need for undercover work or spies. Every child molester would be identified immediately. No double agent could ever get away with it. Psychics would be on demand for high paying jobs in banks, businesses and government. "Most psychics would be very, very rich. . . ." (Radford). And since psychics are such altruistic persons, giving up their time to help others talk to the deceased or figure out what to do with their lives, they would be winning lotteries right and left and giving part of their winnings to help the needy. We wouldn't need trials of accused persons: psychics could tell us who is guilty and who is not. The polygraph would be a thing of the past. Of course, the operative word here is *if*. If psychic power existed the world would be very different.

It seems clear that psychics can be explained in one of three ways: (1) they truly are psychic; (2) they are frauds, taking advantage of people's gullibility and weaknesses; or (3) they're deluded and self-deceived. Of the three options, the least probable is option number one. "Psychics" who are honest about their deception call themselves mentalists and call their art magic or conjuring. Yet, it is the "psychics," not the mentalists, who are the darlings of the mass media. Thus, when the mass media promote "psychics" for their entertainment or news value, they are either promoting fraud or encouraging delusions. Perhaps the media think that because most parties in the psychic game are consenting adults, that makes it ok. Perhaps the police agree and that is why telepsychics like Miss Cleo can practice without fear of arrest.

Further Reading

Alcock, James E., *Science and Supernature: A Critical Appraisal of Parapsychology* (Buffalo, N.Y.: Prometheus Books, 1990).

Blackmore, Susan J., *In Search of the Light: The Adventures of a Parapsychologist* (Buffalo, N.Y.: Prometheus Books, 1986).

Frazier, Kendrick and James Randi, "Predictions After the Fact: Lessons of the Tamara Rand Hoax," in *Science Confronts the Paranormal*, ed., Kendrick Frazier (Buffalo, N.Y.: Prometheus Books, 1986), first published in the *Skeptical Inquirer* 6, no.1 (Fall 1981): 4–7.

Gardner, Martin, *Fads and Fallacies in the Name of Science* (New York: Dover Publications, Inc., 1957), ch. 25.

Gardner, Martin, *How Not to Test a Psychic: Ten Years of Remarkable Experiments with Renowned Clairvoyant Pavel Stepanek* (Buffalo, N.Y.: Prometheus Books, 1989).

Gordon, Henry, *Extrasensory Deception: ESP, Psychics, Shirley MacLaine, Ghosts, UFOs* (Buffalo, N.Y.: Prometheus Books, 1987).

"Guide to 'Cold Reading,'" www.skeptics.com.au/journal/coldread.htm.

Hansel, C.E.M., *The Search for Psychic Power: ESP and Parapsychology Revisited* (Buffalo, N.Y.: Prometheus Books, 1989).

Hyman, Ray, *The Elusive Quarry: A Scientific Appraisal of Psychical Research* (Buffalo, N.Y.: Prometheus Books, 1989).

Keene, M. Lamar, *The Psychic Mafia* (Prometheus, 1997).

Kurtz, Paul, ed., *A Skeptic's Handbook of Parapsychology* (Buffalo, N.Y.: Prometheus Books, 1985).

Marks, David and Richard Kammann, *Psychology of the Psychic* (Buffalo, N.Y.: Prometheus Books, 1979).

Paulos, John Allen, *Innumeracy: Mathematical Illiteracy and Its Consequences* (New York: Vintage Books, 1990).

Radford, Benjamin, "Worlds in Collision: Applying Reality to the Paranormal," *Skeptical Inquirer*, November/December 2000.

Randi, James. *Flim-Flam!* (Buffalo, N.Y.: Prometheus Books, 1982), especially chapter 13, "Put Up or Shut Up," where he gives accounts of tests done on several psychics who have tried to collect the $10,000 Randi used to offer to anyone demonstrating a psychic power. So far, no one has collected, even though the offer is now over $1,000,000!

Rawcliffe, Donovan Hilton, *Occult and Supernatural Phenomena* (New York: Dover Publications, 1988).

Stein, Gordon, "Spiritualism," in *The Encyclopedia of the Paranormal* edited by Gordon Stein (Buffalo, N.Y.: Prometheus Books, 1996).

Steiner, Robert A., "Fortunetelling," in *The Encyclopedia of the Paranormal* edited by Gordon Stein (Buffalo, N.Y.: Prometheus Books, 1996) pp. 281–290.

Stenger, Victor J., *Physics and Psychics: the Search for a World Beyond the Senses* (Buffalo, N.Y.: Prometheus Books, 1990).

Wiseman, Richard, *Deception and Self-Deception: Investigating Psychics* (Buffalo, N.Y.: Prometheus Books, 1997).

Wiseman, Richard and Robert L. Morris, *Guidelines for Testing Psychic Claimants* (Buffalo, N.Y.: Prometheus Books, 1995).

Scientific Experiments Do Not Suggest That Psi Exists

Michael Shermer

Michael Shermer is the publisher of *Skeptic* magazine and the director of the Skeptics Society. He also wrote *Why People Believe Weird Things: Pseudoscience, Superstition, and Other Confusions of Our Time*. In the following selection, Shermer argues that experiments that attempt to prove the existence of extrasensory perception (ESP) are flawed. In any ESP experiment, there will be people who score well below and well above the average for chance. Shermer maintains that these results do not indicate that the test takers have a high degree of ESP ability. Rather, he asserts, probability theory and statistical analysis predict that in any test a small percentage of people will test fairly high and low. The fact that people score as predicted is not a sign of ESP, he concludes.

Excerpted from *From Why People Believe Weird Things: Pseudoscience, Superstition, and Other Confusions of Our Time*, Michael Shermer (New York: W.H. Freeman, 1997). Copyright © 1997 by Michael Shermer. Reprinted by permission of Henry Holt and Company, LLC.

One of the most overused one-liners in the statistical business is Disraeli's classification (and Mark Twain's clarification) of lies into the three taxa "lies, damn lies, and statistics." Of course, the problem really lies in the misuse of statistics and, more generally, in the misunderstanding of statistics and probabilities that most of us have in dealing with the real world. When it comes to estimating the likelihood of something happening, most of us overestimate or underestimate probabilities in a way that can make normal events seem like paranormal phenomena. I saw a classic example of this in a visit to Edgar Cayce's Association for Research and Enlightenment (A.R.E.), located in Virginia Beach, Virginia. One day when I was in town, Clay Drees, a professor at nearby Virginia Wesleyan College, and I decided to pay them a visit. We were fortunate to arrive on a relatively busy day during which the A.R.E. staff were conducting an ESP "experiment" in extrasensory perception (ESP). Since they were claiming that one's ESP could be proved scientifically, we considered A.R.E. fair game for skeptics. . . .

The ESP machine featured the standard Zener cards (created by K.E. Zener, they display easily distinguished shapes to be interpreted in Psi experiments), with a button to push for each of the five symbols—plus sign, square, star, circle, and wavy lines. One of the directors of A.R.E. began with a lecture on ESP, Edgar Cayce, and the development of psychic powers. He explained that some people are born with a psychic gift while others need practice, but we all have the power to some degree. When he asked for participants, I volunteered to be a receiver. I was given no instruction on how to receive psychic messages, so I asked. The instructor explained that I should concentrate on the sender's forehead. The thirty-four other people in the room were told to do the same thing. We were all given an ESP Testing Score Sheet (see figure 1), with paired columns for our psychic choices and the correct answers, given after the experiment. We ran two trials of 25 cards each. I got 7 right in the first set, for which I honestly tried to receive the message, and 3 right in the second set, for which I marked the plus sign for every card.

The Scores

The instructor explained that "5 right is average, chance is between 3 and 7, and anything above 7 is evidence of ESP."

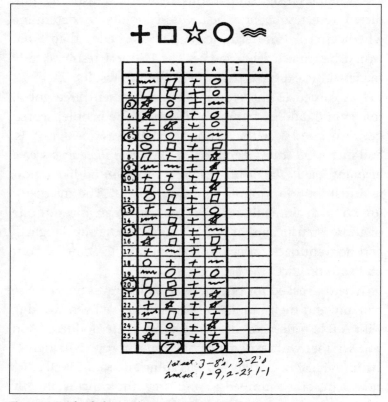

Figure 1: Michael Shermer's ESP Testing Score Sheet.

I asked, "If 3 to 7 is chance, and anything above 7 is evidence of ESP, what about someone who scores below a 3?" The instructor responded, "That's a sign of negative ESP." (He didn't say what that was.) I then surveyed the group. In the first set, three people got 2 right, while another three got 8 right; in the second set, one even got 9 right. So, while I apparently did not have psychic power, at least four other people did. Or did they?

Before concluding that high scores indicate a high degree of ESP ability, you have to know what kind of scores people would get purely by chance. The scores expected by chance can be predicted by probability theory and statistical analysis. Scientists use comparisons between statistically predicted test results and actual test results to determine whether results are significant, that is, better than what would be expected by chance. The ESP test results clearly matched the expected pattern for random results.

I explained to the group, "In the first set, three got 2, three got 8, and everyone else [twenty-nine people] scored between 3 and 7. In the second set, there was one 9, two 2s, and one 1, *all scored by different people than those who scored high and low in the first test!* Doesn't that sound like a normal distribution around an average of 5?" The instructor turned and said, with a smile, "Are you an engineer or one of those statisticians or something?" The group laughed, and he went back to lecturing about how to improve your ESP with practice.

When he asked for questions, I waited until no one else had any and then inquired, "You say you've been working with A.R.E. for several decades, correct?" He nodded. "And you say that with experience one can improve ESP, right?" He immediately saw where I was going and said, "Well . . . ," at which point I jumped in and drew the conclusion, "By now you must be very good at this sort of test. How about we send the signals to you at the machine. I'll bet you could get at least 15 out of the 25." He was not amused at my suggestion and explained to the group that he had not practiced ESP in a long time and, besides, we were out of time for the experiment. He quickly dismissed the group, upon which a handful of people surrounded me and asked for an explanation of what I meant by "a normal distribution around an average of 5."

The Bell Curve

On a piece of scrap paper, I drew a crude version of the normal frequency curve, more commonly known as the bell curve (see figure 2). I explained that the mean, or average number, of correct responses ("hits") is expected by chance

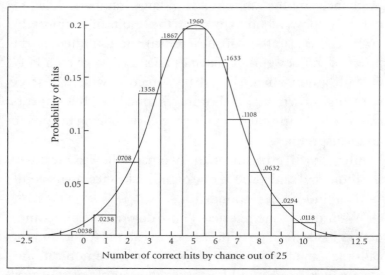

Figure 2: Bell curve for a test of 25 questions with 5 possible answers. If chance is operating, probability predicts that most people (79 percent) will get between 3 and 7 correct, whereas the probability of getting 8 or more correct is 10.9 percent (thus, in a group of 25, several scores in this range will always occur purely by chance), of getting 15 correct is about 1 in 90,000, of getting 20 correct is about 1 in 5 billion, and of getting all 25 correct is about 1 in 300 quadrillion.

to be 5 (5 out of 25). The amount that the number of hits will deviate from the standard mean of 5, by chance, is 2. Thus, for a group this size, we should not put any special significance on the fact that someone got 8 correct or someone scored only 1 or 2 correct hits. This is exactly what is expected to happen by chance.

So these test results suggest that nothing other than chance was operating. The deviation from the mean for this experiment was nothing more than what we would expect. If the audience were expanded into the millions, say on a television show, there would be an even bigger opportunity for misinterpretation of the high scores. In this scenario, a tiny fraction would be 3 standard deviations above the mean, or get 11 hits, a still smaller percentage would reach 4 standard deviations, or 13 hits, and so on, all as predicted by chance and the randomness of large numbers. Believers in psychic power tend to focus on the results of the most deviant subjects (in the statistical sense) and tout them as the proof of the power. But statistics tells us that given a large enough group, there should be someone who will score fairly high. There may be lies and damned lies, but statistics can reveal the truth when pseudoscience is being flogged to an unsuspecting group.

After the ESP experiment, one woman followed me out of the room and said, "You're one of those skeptics, aren't you?"

"I am indeed," I responded.

"Well, then," she retorted, "how do you explain coincidences like when I go to the phone to call my friend and she calls me? Isn't that an example of psychic communication?"

"No, it is not," I told her. "It is an example of statistical coincidences. Let me ask you this: How many times did you go to the phone to call your friend and she did not call? Or how many times did your friend call you but you did not call her first?"

She said she would have to think about it and get back to me. Later, she found me and said she had figured it out: "I only remember the times that these events happen, and I forget all those others you suggested."

"Bingo!" I exclaimed, thinking I had a convert. "You got it. It is just selective perception."

But I was too optimistic. "No," she concluded, "this just proves that psychic power works sometimes but not others."

As James Randi says, believers in the paranormal are like "unsinkable rubber ducks."

Psychics and Mediums Are Frauds

Tony Youens

In the following selection, Tony Youens maintains that most psychics use well-known tricks of the trade, such as asking subtle questions to draw information from the client. The client is then presented with this "psychic knowledge" when in fact the customer, unwittingly or unknowingly, gave the psychic the information in the first place. In addition, most psychics spend much of their sessions in character readings, in which they give mostly flattering portrayals of their client's personality. Furthermore, Youens asserts, most psychic predictions are extremely general in nature and could apply to almost anybody. If the information given by the psychic does not make sense to the client, the psychic can claim that the information is true but the client simply does not understand it. Youens is a safety training officer for Nottingham Trent University in England. He is affiliated with the Association for Skeptical Enquiry and has

From "Before You See a Psychic," by Tony Youens, www.ty.clara.co.uk, July 27, 2001. Copyright © 1998 by Tony Youens. Reprinted with permission.

successfully posed on television as both an astrologer and a
reader of tarot cards.

To the customer the psychic's ability to zero in on their
own particular problem can seem an impressive feat. But
whilst it is sometimes difficult, it is nonetheless possible to
come up with surprisingly accurate information.

Put yourself in the position of the psychic, how could you
possibly home in on a complete stranger's needs without
psychic ability? It seems an impossible task. Well think
about it for a moment. To begin with it is unlikely that the
customer is paying simply out of curiosity. People don't usually have that much money to throw around. So the psychic
can in fact start with a few basic assumptions. Most people
will have a problem that fits broadly into three categories;

• Health
• Wealth
• Relationships

To be honest there isn't much outside these three. Health
might include your own or someone else's. It may range
from serious to something that is simply a figment of the
imagination. Wealth? There is hardly anyone who hasn't got
money worries of some kind. Even if you are rich you might
well be worrying about a dodgy investment, but for most of
us it's the lack of money that causes difficulties. Career and
job prospects can also be included under this heading.

Lastly we come to 'relationships'. This is almost certainly
the best place to start. You could be wondering if you are
going to meet Mr or Mrs Right in the near future. Quite
possibly you are worried about losing your current partner
or, if you have already lost them, wondering if it really is all
over. A powerful reason for wanting guidance is if you are

planning to leave your husband or wife for someone else. A risky step to say the least so you decide to get some psychic assistance. A desire to speak to a dead relative is perhaps another category but can be included under the 'relationships' heading for simplicity. Of course all of these categories can be subdivided further but these three nicely illustrate the basic method.

So the first step for the psychic is to decide which category you come under. The easiest way to find this out is to ask you outright. This may seem a bold step but it will probably appear quite natural, even helpful, to ask you what it is you need guidance on. If you listen to psychics on the radio you will find that most people will ask a direct question such as, "Can you see a relationship for me in the near future?" It may be normal for professional advisers to ask questions but then they don't claim to be psychic.

The psychic can use other clues to help focus their questions in the right area. What clues do they have? After a reading many people will say, "I didn't tell them anything, not a word!" Sometimes they don't have to. They can certainly guess your approximate age. This will help narrow things down. If you are young you are probably not going to be worried about your own health. If you're in your twenties you aren't going to be concerned about your grown up children whereas you might be if you were middle aged. On the other hand an older person might want to get in touch with a dead partner or perhaps be worried about a younger member of the family.

They can also make a mental note of several other things about you. Do you seem confident or shy? Are you smartly dressed or looking a bit hard up? Are you wearing a designer label? How about your voice? Are you well spoken? Do you have a local accent? Is that a wedding or engagement ring? Do you look guilty about something? Are your hands rough or smooth? Is your expensive car parked outside the psychic's house? All these things will give valuable hints and the more people they see the better they will become at guessing correctly.

Using all these clues will help determine the best way to start the reading. Usually though the psychic reader will start with something general. A good opening statement is, "Oh dear you're having a few problems at the moment aren't you." (The tone will be very sympathetic.) It will probably be difficult for the customer to decide whether this is a question or a statement. Even if it is not said as a question it is clear that a response from the customer is required. Another good question is one that might apply to all three of the areas mentioned such as, "You seem uncertain about what course of action you should take. I feel that another person is involved and that's why you're hesitating." This is going to be true of virtually anyone visiting a psychic and the customer will almost certainly give a useful response. The psychic's next move will depend entirely on the customer's reply. If it is confirmed that they are indeed having doubts about something then it's just a matter of moving into the right area. The psychic has a one in three chance (health, wealth, relationships) even if no response is given.

A lot of what psychics give you is known as character reading. They tell you all about yourself which, for the most part, you will probably agree with wholeheartedly. However tests carried out by psychologists would indicate that most people are unable to distinguish a false personality assessment from a genuine one. Particularly if the false one is more flattering. Essentially then this amounts to worthless padding.

For any psychic it's a fairly safe tactic to begin with a character reading before trying to rush in and risk making an embarrassing mistake. This can even be the main part of the whole reading although it may be used as a sort of warming up exercise. For instance a comment on some general character trait as in, "You can appear to most people as very confident but deep down you feel just the opposite" is meant to convince the customer that the psychic has real insight into their character. The character reading will almost certainly contain enough flattery to make acceptance by the customer virtually guaranteed, e.g. "You have a lot of love in you and this isn't always appreciated by those close to you." It's very reassuring to know you're right and everybody else is wrong. Another favourite is, "You're a very spiritual person yourself, quite psychic in many ways. You should try to develop your powers. You're certainly a very caring person. You could be a healer." All very nice and complimentary.

Further development of the reading will depend on the age and sex of the customer, and their marital status. The first two will be obvious and the third if not indicated by a ring will be found out by gentle probing from the psychic.

As an illustration assume the psychic decides to start in the 'relationship' area and thinks the customer is worried about a son or daughter. They are not silly enough to jump in and say, "I see your daughter's playing up again. She's still hanging around with that bloke from the chip shop isn't she?" Instead they will try something a bit more general such as, "I sense some difficulty with a relationship, possibly a younger person." Notice that they are quite vague in their terminology. If it turns out that it's not a son or daughter it would still be correct if they are merely having trouble with someone who is 'a bit younger'. For example if they had argued recently with a younger work colleague.

At this point many people either obligingly jump straight in and confirm that they indeed have a daughter who is being difficult or they give non-verbal clues such as facial expressions which will help the psychic decide if they are on the right track. If there is no response from the customer they might ask directly if there is a problem with a child in the family. They will ask this as though they are simply trying to clarify things (communication with the psychic realm can be difficult after all) and if they are wrong they will open things out a bit by asking if a friend is having this problem. The following imaginary dialogue illustrates this.

Psychic: "I'm getting something to do with a younger person. A problem of some kind is causing family tensions."

Client: Non committal.

Psychic: "Have you a daughter?"

Client: "Yes."

Psychic: "Have you been arguing lately?"

Client: "Well, she just goes out all the time when she should be studying for her exams."

Psychic: "I thought so. I felt a powerful female energy in conflict."

Looking carefully at the psychic's words they never said that;

a) It was a son or daughter—just someone younger.

b) It was family that was being discussed (although it would be logical to assume so) until the psychic asked about a daughter.

c) They had a daughter or even that the customer had been arguing. These were just clarification questions.

Yet many people would say that, "He knew straight away that we'd been arguing and I never said anything. There's no way he could have known." If the client is a woman who looks old enough to have a teenage son or daughter then they almost certainly argue at some time or other. It would be somewhat unusual if they didn't.

Psychics nearly always talk in this vague way. By twisting words and subtly altering their meaning it leaves open lots of ways to get out of a tight spot. If, for example someone had not had a daughter but a son then they might respond with, "Oh I felt that it was a younger person but I also see a girl involved in some way." If their teenage son is having problems with his girlfriend, which is quite possible, the psychic is just as correct.

What's in a Name?

It's always good to get a few names right. This never fails to impress. But what do they say? "Your father's name was George, I believe." Certainly not. The usual method is, once again, to ask questions and then let the customer work out who it might be, e.g.;

- "Why am I getting the name George?"
- "Who's George?"
- "I'm getting the initial 'G'. Does this mean anything to you?"
- "There's a gentleman here called George asking for you."

These phrases are used all the time by spiritualist mediums. The last one is a particular favourite. If it is confirmed Grandad was called George they will say that this is indeed Grandad. If the phrase 'was called George' is used then it can be assumed that Grandad is no longer in the land of the living. However it's not unknown for mediums to get this wrong and assume someone is dead when in fact they are still very much alive. They might say, "He really loved you, didn't he." The customer, slightly surprised replies, "He's still alive!" Without missing a beat they will come back with, "Oh, I know that, dear, but when you were little he really loved you, didn't he. You had a very caring childhood, didn't you."

They get away with this because people think, "Well it can't be easy speaking with the dead can it? They can't be expected to be exactly right all the time." The rationale is that it's probably like listening to a radio with a lot of interference. There are bound to be problems in getting through. So people allow them these little mistakes along the way and after it's all over the customer will probably only remember the things the medium got right anyway. The truth is that it is the customer who comes up with the relationship and the medium simply mentions a name and probably a common one at that.

It's surely reasonable to assume that if they listen to the dead spirit a bit longer they will be able to hear enough to make more sense without constantly asking the customer to fill in the blanks. They can hear the name 'George' over the airwaves so if George keeps shouting (or thinking loudly if it's telepathy) he should be able to say, "I'm her Grandad." Once the customer obligingly confirms things it's remarkable how the crackly psychic line clears up, e.g. The medium says, "Oh yes that's right 'cause he's saying Grandad to me."

This system is routinely used to verify many kinds of information. For example;

"Why am I seeing a red car?"

"Who's having trouble at work?"

"Who recently bought a computer?"

When trying out names the psychic or medium will not always content themselves with offering a single name. They might offer two and if one turns out to be right the other can be conveniently forgotten. An example could be, "Who's Sarah . . . or it might be Sandra? I can't make out if they're friends or. . . ." Now the odds on getting a correct name have just doubled. In a similar vein the psychic may modify a name to make it more likely to fit. "I'm being given the name Edward or maybe it's Ted. . . . Todd?". . .

Tactics for a Successful Reading

The following shows how it is possible to put all this information together and come up with a successful reading.

(Remember though, it will vary depending on the psychic's individual style!)

1. Use general statements or questions.

The question isn't, "Are you thinking of changing jobs?" That's far too obvious. Instead they say, "There's someone close to you thinking of a career change". There's a pause while she waits for your response. It may sound specific but just by using the word 'someone' the whole thing is open to wide interpretation. It's also worth noting the ambiguous phrase 'close to you'. Are they referring to a close member of the family or a colleague who merely sits close by at work? This allows the word 'close' to be interpreted in two slightly different ways and improves the psychic's chances of being correct.

2. Analyse the client's response and modify as necessary.

Taking the above example further. If you know of someone considering a career change then the psychic scores a direct hit. But if it is you that has been thinking of changing jobs, maybe not even seriously, you might well obligingly exclaim, "That's me." Bingo! It's still a direct hit for the psychic. The psychic can then imply that she knew this all the time by adding, "I felt you were looking because. . . ." You might go away with the impression that the psychic knew your innermost thoughts.

But suppose you don't know of anyone who is thinking of changing jobs? It won't matter because whilst you may not know of someone who is considering a career change that doesn't mean it's not so. The obvious conclusion is that the psychic must have some amazing insight. If it is later discovered that someone really is looking to change employment, and this is by no means unlikely, it will only serve to convince you that the psychic is genuine after all.

3. Describe the future.

This is the easy bit because the psychic knows she is on safe ground. It hasn't happened yet so she can't possibly be contradicted. However it still pays the psychic to be vague. Assuming you admit to having toyed with the idea of looking for a new job the psychic can say, "I don't see anything happening immediately but there could be a move in the latter part of this year or may be very early next. The good news is that you'll really love this job and you'll do well. It will certainly mean more money for you . . . blah . . . blah".

This, "I don't see it happening just now but a bit later in the year" approach is widely used. Somehow it sounds convincing. The harsh reality of no immediate benefit mixed with glowing future prospects provides a realistic feel to the reading. This also gives them a time period of about half a year in which to be right and if someone ends up with a new job in that time you could be hooked for life. A variation of this is the, "it will be difficult at first but eventually life will be a bed of roses" approach.

If the psychic adds in some of the other ingredients:
- firing off common names
- asking the client about trivial bits of information, e.g. "Who's having trouble with their washing machine"
- categorising the client and using visual and verbal clues
- use of general information, e.g. the 'bad back' ploy
- dollops of flattery

then a very convincing, but non-psychic, reading is assured.

If You Really Must Visit a Psychic

It is difficult, maybe impossible, to explain in written form all the ruses available to the psychic. However there are certain guidelines that can be followed that will help weed out the more obvious ploys. The following is a list of suggestions which will help you assess the effectiveness of your reading and decide if it was value for money.

Remember these points:

1. The first thing to remember is that all this character

reading stuff is virtually meaningless. It's just padding. Everyone has different facets to their character and at different times we can all be different people. Sometimes we are organised but at other times we can be the complete opposite. Another thing that can be safely ignored is the use of what might be called symbolic language. "I see you at the centre of a great circle and you are drawing others inward. Does this make sense to you?" As ever the poor customer has to do all the work and try to see how this might apply to them. In making guesses the customer will invariably give away more clues which will further assist the psychic.

2. Anyone going to visit a psychic should get agreement first to record the session. *This is an absolute must.* There is *no reason* not to allow this. Some psychics have no objection while others offer feeble excuses like the electrical impulses will interfere with their powers. Not only should this be insisted on but customers should always take along their own tape recorder. Some psychics have suspiciously unreliable equipment, especially if the reading hasn't gone well. Customers who claim that they hardly said a word and gave the psychic no clues can be amazed when they play back the tape and find just how much information they gave away.

3. Don't offer information. They are supposed to be telling, not asking. Nevertheless they will ask a surprising number of questions if they can get away with it. People want a successful reading and therefore don't want to be seen as being unhelpful and blocking the psychic's supposed power, so they go along with the questions in the spirit of co-operation. The ever helpful customer acknowledges even semi-correct statements immediately, when if they had waited they might have found that the psychic, not getting the required response covered their options with a suitable get out.

The supposed power of the psychic actually comes from

interaction with you. In fact Tarot readers usually emphasise the importance of your interpretation of how the cards apply to you. Someone who refuses to answer questions and remains poker faced throughout will receive a much poorer reading. If you are with a real psychic surely this would not be the case. Afterwards you can go through the reading and count how many questions were actually asked (don't forget that anything that provokes you into giving a response should count as a question). You can also try to notice how the medium modified his or her statements in light of your response. This can be difficult at first but the more you listen to readings the better you get at spotting their techniques.

4. Finally, ask them what they can actually do. Saying that they are 'psychic' doesn't really tell you very much. What do they claim to be able to do? (If it's character analysis forget it.) Can they foretell the future? Can they get information from a dead relative? Telling you, "Aunt Freda sends her love and is thinking of you" is easy. What about her secret recipe for elderberry wine or where she's hidden her will? Can they locate your missing relative? If you find out exactly what they can do, then you will have some means of measuring their success later. But remember when you are trying to find out how good they are, think about all the times they were wrong and compare this with the number of times they appeared to be correct. Finding Aunt Freda's will under the mattress isn't so clever if you were also told to look down the back of the sofa, in the shed, at a local solicitors, behind the picture on the mantle piece and somewhere on the bookshelf.

Little Evidence Supports Psychic Healing

Christopher French

Christopher French is a senior lecturer in psychology, parapsychology, and pseudoscience at Goldsmiths College at the University of London in England. In his essay on psychic healing, which originally appeared in *The Encyclopedia of the Paranormal*, French discusses the emergence of psychic healing in the alternative health movement. Although many psychic healers claim to have cured seriously ill patients, there is no medically documented proof that psychic healing cured the patients. In many cases, the patients were not truly ill; in others, the patients temporarily felt better and attributed the improvement to psychic healing. However, French notes, feeling better is not the same as becoming well. French believes that many psychic healing "cures" are actually due to the placebo effect, in which the patient's suffering is alleviated because he or she believes in the treatment. While psychic healers may make their patients feel

From "Psychic Healing," by Christopher French, *The Encyclopedia of the Paranormal*, edited by Gordon Stein (Amherst, NY: Prometheus, 1996). Copyright © 1996 by Gordon Stein. Reprinted by permission of Prometheus Books.

better temporarily, there is little evidence to support their claims of cures. However, French concludes that when psychic healers treat people who are genuinely ill they can cause more harm than good by keeping them from receiving truly effective and possibly lifesaving help.

Psychic healing refers to an alleged ability to treat illness by exerting a paranormal influence without using physical curative agents of any kind. Psychic healing may also be known as mental healing, spiritual healing, faith healing, psi healing, divine healing, miracle healing, paranormal healing, laying-on of hands, nonmedical healing, shamanistic healing, and by various other names, although these terms are not completely interchangeable. It is claimed that psychic healing can take place in different ways, sometimes with the healer actually physically near to the patient, perhaps touching the patient's body lightly or else passing his or her hands over the body without touching it. Some psychic healers claim to be able to treat illnesses at a distance and even to be able to treat patients effectively when the patients themselves have not been told that any psychic healing was to take place. For the purposes of this article, the term "healer" is used to refer to those who claim that they heal by paranormal means. This should not be taken to imply that practitioners of conventional medicine, generally referred to here as "doctors," do not heal their patients in the more general sense of the word. . . .

The Nature of Disease
If one receives a particular treatment for a particular illness and one starts to feel better, it is very natural to assume that the treatment caused the improvement. It is also very wrong

to do so. A consideration of the nature of disease shows why it would be wrong to make such an assumption (see also Hines 1988; Buckman and Sabbagh 1993) and why properly controlled clinical trials are an essential part of establishing the validity of any treatment. Diseases—even serious diseases—rarely manifest themselves as a relentless decline into death. Instead, it is far more likely that patients will experience fluctuations in their illness, even if the overall trend, as in the case of terminal diseases, is downward. Some serious illnesses, such as arthritis and multiple sclerosis, are renowned for their extreme variability over time. It is understandable that those suffering from diseases will tend to seek help from unorthodox medical sources when the disease has been getting worse for a period and conventional approaches to treatment seem to have failed. It is quite likely that precisely at such times, due to the natural variability in the course of diseases, the illness will show a temporary improvement, convincing the patient that the therapy caused the improvement.

Most clients who seek out psychic healers do not, of course, suffer from terminal or chronic illnesses. Terrence Hines (1988) estimates that around three-quarters of patients presenting themselves for treatment are suffering from self-limiting ailments, that is, relatively minor complaints that will clear up on their own, thanks to the body's natural defenses. Once again, however, patients may well feel inclined to attribute any improvement to whatever treatment they have had if the treatment is followed by the improvement. If, following the application of a new type of treatment, all patients suffering from a certain disease have recovered within two weeks, this might initially strike one as a useful discovery. If you then learn that the disease in question was the common cold, the importance of taking the body's natural recuperative abilities into account becomes obvious.

From consideration of the two factors just outlined, that is, the inevitable fluctuations in the course of disease and the self-limiting nature of most diseases, it is apparent that one must always evaluate treatments by comparing the treated group with an untreated (or control) group. If it is demonstrated that the treated group has improved relative to the untreated group, then you might feel that you could at last have some faith in the therapeutic effectiveness of your treatment. Unfortunately, you would still be mistaken because you have not yet taken placebo effects into account.

Placebo Effects

Placebo effects can be defined as "any useful effects accompanying some form of treatment that are not directly due to the treatment itself acting on the disease or the patient" (Buckman and Sabbagh 1993, 174). It is useful at this point to emphasize a distinction that is sometimes made between disease, which may be defined as the existence of a pathological process, and illness, which may be defined as how people feel regarding their health. The two terms, although often used interchangeably, are not in fact synonymous as these definitions make clear. A person may have a disease (e.g., high blood pressure), but not feel at all ill. Alternatively, a person may feel ill but not be suffering from any recognized disease. According to Petr Skrabanek and J. McCormick (1990), "Placebos have no effect on the progress or outcome of disease, but they may exert a powerful effect upon the subjective phenomena of illness, pain, discomfort, and distress. Their success is based upon this fact" (13–14).

It is well recognized within medicine that if a group of patients suffering from some painful condition are given pills that contain no active ingredient whatsoever, but are told that the pills are powerful painkillers, a large proportion (typically at least a third) will report that their pain has indeed lessened. It would be a mistake to infer from this that their pain was in some sense imaginary in the first place. The experience of pain is a complex phenomenon. Injuries sustained in battle are often borne with little apparent discomfort, where the same injuries in civilian life would have the sufferer writhing in agony. Presumably the prospect of leaving the battlefield provides enough relief to the injured soldier that the injury itself is not perceived as so severe. Context and expectations are all-important in pain perception. Other subjective symptoms, including sleeplessness, nausea, and depression, may also respond positively to treatments that are in fact therapeutically worthless. . . .

Reviewing the Evidence

Space limitations preclude a detailed review of studies that have attempted to investigate psychic healing in humans under controlled conditions. Instead, the conclusions of three recent reviews of the area will be considered. It is useful to consider here two separate questions relating to psychic healing. First, how good is the evidence that psychic healers can heal? Second, how convincing is the evidence that any healing effects are mediated by paranormal forces?

J. Solfvin (1984) concluded his review as follows:

> In summary, the studies reviewed here show a rather high rate of success for observing, with varying degrees of control, apparent influences on living matter in mental healing contexts. This is very encouraging in that it represents a solid first step toward building a science of mental healing, or mental intention to heal. It is clear, too, that it is only a first step. Many basic questions, such as "what caused these effects," "is psi operating here," and "how can we best model and research these phenomena," are yet to be answered. (63)

Clearly, Solfvin is not convinced that paranormal forces are involved in so-called psychic healing.

Daniel J. Benor (1990) adopts a "head-counting" approach to the studies of psychic healing that he reviews, pointing out that significant effects were obtained in 77 out of 131 "controlled trials." He continues:

> Though many studies are flawed in minor aspects and some flawed in major ways, there still remains a convincing number of excellent experiments with significant results. If healing were a drug, I believe it would be accepted as effective on the basis of this evidence. (30)

It should be noted that Benor's (1990) review deals predominantly with studies of claimed healing effects upon nonhuman tissue. Benor rightly points out that if significant effects are found in such studies, they cannot be due to placebo effects (although, of course, they may still be due to other uncontrolled aspects of the experimental design). . . . Having said that, there are problems in assessing the validity of Benor's conclusions that apply as strongly to the thirty-seven studies involving human healing as to the ninety-four involving nonhuman living tissue in his review. Essentially, Benor gives as much weight to poorly controlled studies as to apparently more rigorous ones. Exceptional claims demand exceptionally high-quality evidence and the piling up of results from poorly conducted studies is no substitute. The history of science is littered with episodes of "pathological science" during which hundreds of papers have been published on phenomena that subsequently turned out to be entirely illusory (e.g., N-rays, polywater; see, e.g., Hines 1988). Many of the studies reviewed by Benor are unreplicated and possibly unreplicable. Much of the work he refers to has been published in obscure journals with unknown standards of peer review. It might be objected that these criticisms are unfair given that Benor does not claim to have presented an exhaustive critical assessment in this single review article. In fact, however, the same criticisms can be directed at his book-length reviews (e.g., Benor 1993).

Subjective Effects

The final review to be considered is that of S.A. Schouten (1992–1993). Schouten writes as follows:

> An overview of the research on the effectiveness of "psychic" healing on human subjects indicates that psychic healing can be effective, especially on subjectively experienced state of health. Objectively measured effects are much less pronounced. However, the strength of the effect of psychic healing seems strongly dependent upon the patient's knowledge that treatment is attempted and appears to be mainly related to psychological variables associated with the patient and with the healer-patient interaction. (35)

Schouten is clearly emphasizing the role played by placebo effects in subjectively experienced improvements and pointing to the dearth of convincing evidence relating to objectively measured improvements. The patients are not as ill, in that they feel better, but the disease process itself is generally unaltered. There is a big difference between feeling better and getting better.

It should be noted that all of the reviews referred to here were written by individuals who accept that paranormal forces do exist. It cannot therefore be objected that Schouten and Solfvin adopted a prejudiced approach to the data base. Only Benor finds the evidence for a paranormal effect convincing and even he recognizes that many of the studies were flawed. Schouten (1992–1993) points out that psychic healing is an effective form of treatment if one accepts the not unreasonable position that placebo effects are examples of effective healing. There is no need, however, to invoke a paranormal explanation of the healing effects produced and, besides, it is difficult to see how a paranormal explanation could apply. As Schouten, who believes in psi, writes,

> Although experimental evidence suggests the existence of a paranormal anomalous effect, the size of the effect is small compared to the effects observed in psychic healing. In the

case of many complaints, it is also unclear how a possible paranormal effect could result in an improvement in health. Hence, although the possible contribution of a paranormal process cannot be excluded, it is unlikely to account for the observed effects of psychic healing on patients. (35)

In answer to the questions posed earlier, we can conclude as follows. If we include placebo effects in our definition of healing, then psychic healers can heal. If we adopt a definition of healing as meaning therapeutic effectiveness over and above the placebo effect, the evidence that psychic healers can heal is much less convincing, even to many commentators with a generally sympathetic attitude towards psi. It follows that there is no need to invoke paranormal forces to explain the healing achieved by psychic healers in well-controlled studies. . . .

The Need for Medical Evidence

James Randi (1987) rightly emphasizes the need for good medical evidence relating to the patient's health before and after any alleged cure. It is often the case that patients do not have the disease that they think they have. For example, Peter May, M.D., challenged Morris Cerullo, an American evangelical faith healer, to produce details of his "best cases" during Cerullo's "Mission to London" in 1992 (May 1993–1994). Among the cases produced, none of which provided convincing evidence for faith healing, was that of Georgine McHale, a 46-year-old woman who claimed to have been cured of a fibroid. In fact, her medical records revealed no mention of a fibroid having actually been diagnosed. Instead, they showed that a test had been arranged to investigate the possibility of a fibroid. The test, carried out three weeks after the alleged cure, showed two ovarian cysts, but no fibroid. May also provides details of cases where the patients really did have the medical problems that they thought they had (e.g., spinal degeneration, poor vision, hip displacement), but that they still had them after the alleged miracle cures. In one particularly tragic case, a little girl named Natalia Barned was declared cured of "cancer of the blood and the bones" by Cerullo and made to run about the stage. She died two months later.

There are many ways in which patients might be misled regarding their diagnosis. Human beings are imperfect information processors even at the best of times. In the stressful situation of the doctor's office misunderstandings are a common occurrence. It is not surprising that patients can get the wrong idea concerning their diagnosis and/or prognosis. In some cases, the patient's illness has never been diagnosed by a qualified doctor, but instead by the healer himself or herself. It is worth noting too that systematic studies have shown that, not surprisingly, even conventional doctors sometimes misdiagnose their patients (see Buckman and Sabbagh 1993). They are only human after all. This suggests that Randi (1987) would be unwise to accept a single case meeting his criteria as providing conclusive evidence for the reality of faith healing. Having said that, he has yet to find such a case.

Randi (1987) also raises the issue of simultaneous conventional medical treatment. P. May (1993–1994) provides the following example of an individual whom Cerullo claimed to have cured of esophageal cancer: "Alfred Coombes was an elderly man who claimed to have been healed of a malignancy in his gullet. He readily admitted that he had just had a course of fifteen sessions of radiotherapy, and thanked God for the skill of his doctors" (8). . . .

James Randi (1987), a highly skilled conjuror himself, has done much to reveal the techniques employed. The Reverend W.V. Grant, for example, gives the impression that God has revealed information to him about the people at his faith healing rallies. He appears to know their names, their illnesses, and much more, and yet they have never spoken to him before. What is not so obvious, however, is that they have spoken to Grant's staff, who pump them for information and report it back to Grant before the show begins. Peter Popoff used a much more sophisticated method. He had his wife relay the information to him via a tiny radio receiver in his ear. This trick was exposed when Randi, with the aid of a communications specialist, managed to record Popoff's wife feeding him the information during a service. Many other tricks are used to give the impression that miracle cures are being performed when in fact they are not (see Randi 1987 for details). The main motivation is greed. The most successful faith healers in America are millionaires many times over having convinced their flocks, predominantly the poor and the elderly, that they have a direct line to the Almighty.

Real Dangers

While it is obvious that no one would approve of such immoral activities, does it generally do any harm to allow the more typical self-proclaimed psychic healers to provide whatever comfort they can to the sick? This is not an easy question to answer. As stated earlier, the placebo effect has the potential to alleviate many types of suffering, and alternative therapists are actually in a better position to exploit it than conventional doctors. This is because they usually have great faith in their own particular form of therapy, whereas conventional doctors are all too aware of the limitations of orthodox medicine. Moreover, they are professionally bound to tell their patients about these limitations. This in itself is likely to reduce the placebo effect. It is also true that conventional doctors generally have a lot to learn from alternative practitioners regarding healer-patient relationships. Conventional medicine is often perceived to be cold and impersonal.

It is undoubtedly the case, however, that there are real dangers when psychic healing is relied upon to the exclusion of conventional medicine. Members of the Church of Christ, Scientist, for example, are forbidden from treating illness other than by "the power of prayer." Even worse, children of the sect members are also forbidden treatment, and many have died as a direct consequence (Hines 1988). There can be no excuses for such avoidable tragedies in the modern world.

Bibliography

Benor, Daniel J. "Survey of Spiritual Healing Research." *Complementary Medical Research* 4 (1990): 9–33.

―――. *Healing Research: Holistic Energy Medicine and Spirituality.* Vol. 1. Deddington, Oxon, U.K.: Helix, 1993.

Buckman, Rob, and K. Sabbagh. *Magic or Medicine? An Investigation into Healing.* London: Macmillan, 1993.

Hines, Terrence. *Pseudoscience and the Paranormal: A Critical Examination of the Evidence.* Amherst, N.Y.: Prometheus Books, 1988.

May, P. "The Faith Healing Claims of Morris Cerullo." *Free Inquiry* (Winter 1993–1994): 5–11.

Nolen, William A. *Healing: A Doctor in Search of a Miracle.* New York: Random House, 1974.

Randi, James. *The Faith Healers.* Amherst, N.Y.: Prometheus Books, 1987.

Schouten, S.A. "Psychic Healing and Complementary Medicine." *European Journal of Parapsychology* 9 (1992–1993): 35–91.

Skrabanek, Petr, and J. McCormick. *Follies and Fallacies in Medicine.* Amherst, N.Y.: Prometheus Books, 1990.

Solfvin, J. "Mental Healing." In *Advances in Parapsychological Research.* vol. 4., edited by S. Krippner, 31–63. Jefferson, N.C.: McFarland and Company, 1984.

The Success of Remote Viewing Does Not Indicate the Existence of Psi

Ray Hyman

Ray Hyman is a professor of psychology at the University of Oregon and a member of the executive council of the Center for the Scientific Investigation of Claims of the Paranormal (CSICOP). He was one of two experts hired by the CIA in 1995 to evaluate the remote-viewing program for the agency. In the following viewpoint, Hyman argues that although the ten remote viewing experiments the panel examined for the CIA's report had a "hit" rate that was higher than average, that is not proof that psychic ability was responsible for the success of the experiments. He asserts that ESP can be credited only when every other normal explanation has been ruled out. The experiments' success can only be acknowledged when independent laboratories have

From "Evaluation of the Military's Twenty-Year Program on Psychic Spying," by Ray Hyman, *Skeptical Inquirer*, March/April 1996. Copyright © 1996 by *Skeptical Inquirer*. Reprinted with permission.

replicated the experiments and when science is able to devise a positive test showing when psi is present rather than when it is not.

In the early 1970s the Central Intelligence Agency supported a program to see if a form of extrasensory perception (ESP) called "remote viewing" could assist with intelligence gathering. The program consisted of laboratory studies conducted at Stanford Research Institute (SRI) under the direction of Harold Puthoff and Russel Targ. In addition to the laboratory research, psychics were employed to provide information on targets of interest to the intelligence community.

Stargate

The CIA abandoned this program in the late 1970s because it showed no promise. The Defense Intelligence Agency (DIA) took over the program and continued supporting it until it was suspended in the spring of 1995. Under the DIA the program was named Stargate and consisted of three components. One component kept track of what foreign countries were doing in the area of psychic warfare and intelligence gathering. A second component, called the "Operations Program," involved six, and later three, psychics on the government payroll who were available to any government agency that wanted to use their services. The third component was the laboratory research on psychic phenomena first carried out at SRI and later transferred to Science Applications International Corporation (SAIC) in Palo Alto, California.

This program was secret until it was declassified in early 1995. The declassification was done to enable an outside evaluation of the program. Because of some controversies within the program, a Senate committee decided to transfer the program from the DIA back to the CIA. The CIA, before deciding the fate of the program, contracted with the American Institutes for Research (A.I.R.), Washington, D.C., to conduct the evaluation. The A.I.R. hired Jessica Utts, a statistician at the University of California at Davis, and me, a psychologist at the University of Oregon, as the evaluation panel.

The idea was to have a balanced evaluation by hiring an expert who was known to support the reality of psychic phenomena and one who was skeptical about the existence of psi. Utts, in addition to being a highly regarded statistician, has written and argued for the existence of psychic phenomena and has been a consultant to the SRI and SAIC remote-viewing experiments.

Most recently, I served on the National Research Council committee that issued a report stating that the case for psychic phenomena had no scientific justification (*Skeptical Inquirer*, Fall 1988). In the January 1995 issue of *Psychological Bulletin* I supplied a skeptical commentary on the article by Daryl Bem and Charles Honorton that argued that the recent ganzfeld studies provided evidence for replicable experiments on ESP (See *Skeptical Inquirer*, Fall 1985).

At the beginning of last summer, Utts and I were each supplied with copies of all the reports that had been generated by the remote-viewing program during the 20 years of its existence. This consisted of three large cartons of documents.

We met with Edwin May, the principal investigator who took over this remote-viewing research project (after Puthoff and Targ left SRI in the 1980s); representatives of the CIA; and representatives of A.I.R. The purpose of the meeting was to coordinate our efforts as well as to focus our efforts on those remote-viewing studies that offered the most promise of being scientifically respectable. May helped identify the ten best studies for Utts and me to evaluate.

While Utts and I focused on the best laboratory studies, the two psychologists from A.I.R. conducted an evaluation of the recent operational uses of the three remote viewers (psychics) then on the government payroll. We all agreed that any scientifically meaningful evaluation of these operational psychic intelligence uses was impossible. The operational program had been kept separate from the laboratory research, and the work of the remote viewers was conducted in ways that precluded meaningful evaluation. Nevertheless, we all cooperated in developing a structured interview that the A.I.R. staff could use on the program officer, the three psychics, and the individuals or agencies that had used the services of these remote viewers.

The users said, through the interviews, that the remote viewers did not supply information that was useful in intelligence or other contexts.

The Experiments

The remote-viewing experiments that Utts and I evaluated had, for the most part, been conducted since 1986 and presumably had been designed to meet the objections that the National Research Council and other critics had aimed at the remote-viewing experiments conducted before 1986. These experiments varied in a number of ways but the typical experiment had these components:

1. The remote viewers were always selected from a small pool of previously "successful" viewers. May emphasized that, in his opinion, this ability is possessed by approximately one in every 100 persons. Therefore, they used the same set of "gifted" viewers in each experiment.

2. The remote viewer would be isolated with an experimenter in a secure location. At another location, a sender would look at a target that had been randomly chosen from

a pool of targets. The targets were usually pictures taken from the *National Geographic*. During the sending period the viewer would describe and draw whatever impressions came to mind. After the session, the viewer's description and a set of five pictures (one of them being the actual target picture) would be given to a judge. The judge would then decide which picture was closest to the viewer's description. If the actual target was judged closest to the description, this was scored as a "hit."

In this simplified example I have presented, we would expect one hit by chance 20 percent of the time. If a viewer consistently scored more hits than chance, this was taken as evidence for psychic functioning. This description captures the spirit of the experimental evidence although I have simplified matters for convenience of exposition. In fact, the judging was somewhat more complex and involved rank ordering each potential target against the description.

A hit rate better than the chance baseline of 20 percent can be considered evidence for remote viewing, of course, only if all other nonpsychic possibilities have been eliminated. Obvious nonpsychic possibilities would be inadequacies of the statistical model, inadequacies of the randomization procedure in selecting targets or arranging them for judging, sensory leakage from target to viewer *or* from target to judge, and a variety of other sources of bias.

The elimination of these sources of above-chance hitting is no easy task. The history of psychical research and parapsychology presents example after example of experiments that were advertised as having eliminated all nonpsychic possibilities and that were discovered by subsequent investigators to have had subtle and unsuspected biases. Often it takes years before the difficulties with a new experimental design or program come to light.

Utts and I submitted separate evaluations. We agreed that

the newly unclassified experiments seemed to have eliminated the obvious defects of the earlier remote-viewing experiments. We also agreed that these ten best experiments
were producing hit rates consistently above the chance baseline. We further agreed that a serious weakness of this set of
studies is the fact that only one judge, the principal investigator, was used in all the remote-viewing experiments. We
agreed that these results remain problematical until it can
be demonstrated that significant hitting will still occur
when independent judges are used.

Beyond this we disagreed dramatically. Utts concluded
that these results, when taken in the context of other contemporary parapsychological experiments—especially the
ganzfeld experiments—prove the existence of psychic functioning. I find it bizarre to jump from these cases of statistically significant hitting to the conclusion that a paranormal
phenomenon has been proven. As I pointed out, we both
agreed that the results of the new remote-viewing experiments have to be independently judged. If independent
judges cannot produce the same significant hit rates, this
alone would suffice to discard these experiments as evidence of psychic abilities. More to the point, just because
these experiments are less than 10 years old and have only
recently been opened to public scrutiny, we do not know if
they contain hidden and subtle biases or if they can be independently replicated in other laboratories. The history of
parapsychology is replete with "successful" experiments
that subsequently could not be replicated.

Utts is obviously impressed with consistencies between
the new remote-viewing experiments and the current
ganzfeld experiments. Where she sees consistencies, I see inconsistencies. The ganzfeld experiments all use the subjects
as their own judges. The claim is that the results do not
show up when independent judges are used. The exact op-

posite is true of remote-viewing experiments. When subjects are used as their own judges in remote-viewing experiments, the outcome is rarely, if ever, successful. Successful results come about only when the judges are someone other than the remote viewer. The recent ganzfeld experiments get successful results only with dynamic (animated video clips) rather than static targets. The remote-viewing experiments mostly use static targets. I could go on spelling out such inconsistencies, but this would be futile.

Even if the consistent hit rate above chance can be replicated with independent remote-viewing experiments, this would be a far cry from having demonstrated something paranormal. Parapsychologist John Palmer has argued that the successful demonstration of an above-chance statistical anomaly is insufficient to prove a paranormal cause. This is because remote viewing and ESP are currently only defined negatively. ESP is what is left after the experimenter has eliminated all obvious, normal explanations.

A Negative Definition

Several problems are created by trying to establish the existence of a phenomenon on the basis of a negative definition. For one thing, if ESP is shown by any departure from chance that has no obvious normal explanation, there is no way to show that the observed departures are due to one or several causes. Also, the claim for psi can never be falsified, because any glitch in the data can be used as evidence for psi. What is needed, of course, is a positive theory of psychic functioning that enables us to tell *when psi is present* and *when it is absent*. As far as I can tell, every other discipline that claims to be a science deals with phenomena whose presence or absence can clearly be decided.

The evidence for N-rays, mitogenetic radiation, polywater, cold fusion, and a host of other "phenomena" that no longer are considered to exist was much clearer and stronger than the current evidence for psychic functioning. In these cases of alleged phenomena, at least we were given criteria to decide when the reputed phenomena were supposed to be present and when they were not. Nothing like this exists in parapsychology. Yet the claim is being made that a phenomenon has been clearly demonstrated.

Fortunately, we do not have to squabble over whether the current remote-viewing experiments do or do not prove the existence of an anomalous phenomenon. We can follow the normal and accepted scientific process of (1) waiting to see if independent laboratories can replicate the above chance hitting conditions using appropriate controls; (2) seeing whether the researchers can devise positive tests to enable us to decide when psi is present and when it is absent; (3) seeing whether they can specify conditions under which we can reliably observe the phenomenon; (4) showing that the phenomenon varies in lawful ways with specifiable variables. Every science—except parapsychology—has met this accepted procedure. So far, parapsychology has not even come close to meeting any of these criteria. It is premature to draw any conclusions. We will simply have to wait and see. If history is a guide, then this will be a long wait, indeed.

Epilogue: Analyzing the Evidence

Humans have believed in the paranormal for thousands of years. One of the first written records of a test of paranormal powers occurred during the reign of Croesus, the king of Lydia from 560 to 546 B.C. Croesus had an important question about the future he needed answered, but he did not know which of seven oracles could be believed. So he devised a test for them. Croesus sent messengers to the seven oracles, all of whom were asked to describe what the king was doing on a certain day. Only one, the Oracle of Delphi, answered the query correctly, describing the activity of making a stew of lamb and tortoise meat in a bronze pot: "A tortoise boiling with a lamb I smell: Bronze underlies and covers them as well."[1] Now that Croesus had identified an oracle whose answers he could trust, he asked the one question he really wanted answered: Would he be victorious if he went to Persia and attacked Cyrus? The oracle answered, "When Croesus has the Halys crossed, a mighty empire will be lost."[2] Unfortunately for Croesus, he did not ask the oracle which empire, and it was his own that would be lost in the battle.

When Croesus devised his test for the oracles, he followed one of the most important guidelines that modern science has since set for any experiment testing psychic abilities: Make sure there is no possibility of "leakage"—that is, that there is no way that the subject being tested could peek, use the process of elimination, or use visual or verbal cues from the tester or surroundings to determine the correct answer. Croesus did not tell his messengers what he planned to do on the day in question, so there was no way that the messengers could give any kind of a clue to the oracles. And to lessen the chance that an oracle might give the correct answer simply by coincidence, Croesus chose an activity, cooking, that was decidedly unkinglike. He knew that anyone who correctly described what he was doing truly had psychic powers and was not simply guessing or playing the odds.

However, many scientists would say that the Delphi oracle's extrasensory perception—both clairvoyance (seeing the king make his lamb-and-tortoise stew) and precognition (foretelling the outcome of the battle)—contradicts the laws of nature and is therefore physically impossible. Physicist Milton Rothman, author of *A Physicist's Guide to Skepticism*, believes that all activities—normal and paranormal— must follow physical principles:

> Transmission of information through space requires transfer of energy from one place to another. Telepathy requires transmission of an energy-carrying signal directly from one mind to another. All descriptions of ESP imply violations of conservation of energy [the principle that mass energy can be neither created nor destroyed] in one way or another, as well as violations of all the principles of information theory and even of the principle of causality [the principle that an effect cannot precede its cause]. Strict application of physical principles requires us to say that ESP is impossible.[3]

However, there have been many instances in which scientists have proclaimed some idea to be impossible that was later proven otherwise. For example, in 1772 the French Academy of Sciences refused to accept the possibility of meteorites, declaring that "the falling of stones from the sky is physically impossible."[4] Today, of course, it is universally accepted that meteorites fall to the earth on a regular basis.

Scientific advances only come when scientists attempt to explain anomalous events—events that do not seem to obey the known laws of nature. For example, the old theory did not accept the falling of stones from the sky, but stones continued to fall; as a result, a new theory had to be found that included the existence of meteors. Those who study psychic phenomena contend that the same goes for ESP. If the natural law that suggests that ESP is impossible is flawed, then ESP may indeed be possible.

One argument that both skeptics and supporters of paranormal phenomena use to promote their theories is "negative evidence." Those who use this argument use a lack of evidence—either pro or con—to support their contention. For example, parapsychologists may claim that, since there is no proof that psi—a term used to indicate extrasensory perception and psychokinesis—does not exist, then it must exist. Conversely, skeptics often try to use the argument that, since a phenomenon has not been proven to exist, it must not exist.

Many scientists refuse to consider the possibility of psi when examining paranormal phenomena, and some experts claim this is because accepting the existence of psi would change the basic assumptions of science. Richard S. Broughton, director of research at the Institute of Parapsychology, explains:

> Parapsychological hypotheses at the very least claim that humans can acquire information or affect external physical systems in ways that science, in its present state, cannot explain. If these claims are correct, then the existing worldview that science gives us will have to be modified—the so-called laws of physics will have to be rewritten.[5]

Explaining Anomalous Behavior

Sometimes laws of nature must be rewritten, but skeptical researchers make every attempt to eliminate any and all possible explanations for anomalous behavior before they will even consider such a drastic step. In the case of psi, Broughton notes,

The pivotal point about which the entire parapsychological controversy turns is whether or not "normal explanations," which are compatible with the existing worldview, have really been excluded for any given parapsychological claim or experimental result. Could the subjects in researcher X's experiment in fact have obtained the information through some normal means? Did subject Y have an opportunity to cheat in such-and-such an experiment? This is where scientific control becomes so important.[6]

Believers in psi attempt to impose strict scientific controls on their experiments to avoid cheating and fraud and to satisfy skeptics, but because of their belief, they may be predisposed to see psychic activity where none exists.

Researchers have documented that belief is an important factor to consider in the debate over psychic phenomena. Broughton writes,

If a person's *a priori* conviction is that psi phenomena cannot possibly exist, then any "normal" explanation, no matter how bizarre and convoluted it might have to be, will be preferable to an explanation that invokes psi phenomena.[7]

Those who believe in the possibility of psi tend to perform well on psychic ability tests, typically scoring better than chance would dictate. Those who are skeptical of psi tend to do worse on psychic tests than the laws of probability would predict. These tendencies tend to exist whether those taking the tests are the experiments' subjects or researchers. Susan Blackmore, a scientist who is highly skeptical of psychic phenomena, has attempted to replicate the test results of several parapsychologists who reported successful psi experiments. Blackmore's tests have never indicated any existence of psi, however. This could be because psi does not exist, because her test subjects are not psychic, or, as some allege, because her skeptical mind has a "polluting effect"[8] on psychic activity.

To explain psi and its apparent contradiction of known

physical laws, some scientists have delved into quantum mechanics. The theory underlying quantum mechanics—which studies subatomic matter—is that everything is indelibly connected in some mysterious way. For example, when an electron collides with its opposite, a positron, each is destroyed, but in the process two photons are created. Neither of these photons has any properties, such as a charge or velocity, until it is seen by an observer. Then, the very act of noting the presence of the photon assigns it a certain spin (charge). At the exact moment that photon A acquires its spin, photon B, no matter how far away it is from photon A, begins spinning in the opposite direction. Despite having no physical connection to the first photon, the second photon seems to instantly "know" what has happened and responds accordingly. Some researchers maintain that this occurrence suggests that the human subconscious may be a part of this universal interconnectedness, allowing people to communicate telepathically.

Why Mainstream Science Does Not Accept Parapsychology

The primary impediment to the scientific acceptance of psi is the fact that most psi experiences cannot be replicated in the laboratory and tested to see if there are other possible explanations for the phenomena. Most psychic phenomena are fleeting; they do not last long enough for scientists to be summoned, set up their equipment, and begin testing for psi. In addition, many experiments on psychic phenomena are filled with errors, sloppy procedures that permit leakage, and sometimes even fraud, in which the researchers manipulate the results to support their theories. Author Upton Sinclair studied psychic phenomena extensively with his wife, Mary Craig, who believed she had telepathic powers. "The factor which makes psychic phenomena so hard for the scientific world to accept," he wrote, "is cheating." However, Sinclair voiced the opinions of many when he wrote, "There is no power of man which may not and will not be abused. In spite of all fraud, I am convinced that there are thousands of genuine clairvoyants and psychics."[9]

There are many ways in which psychics or researchers can manipulate the results of psi experiments. For example, researchers may have performed experiments that did not give the results that were expected or desired. The reports of these experiments are not published but filed away, never to be seen again. This is known as the "file drawer" problem. Skeptics often argue that if all the failed experiments that have been filed away are added in with the successful experiments, then the results of all the studies combined would look more like chance. Parapsychologists counter that their field is very small, with very few researchers performing experiments. The number of file drawer studies needed to balance experiments that support the existence of psi is impossible: There are not enough researchers to have performed that many experiments.

The Ganzfeld Showdown

The file drawer problem played a role in the ganzfeld experiments analyzed by Charles Honorton. Parapsychologists Honorton, Carl Sargent, and others performed many ganzfeld experiments (an experiment in which the subject describes an image that is being sent telepathically by a person in another room) that yielded similar results. In 1981, Honorton did a metanalysis of all the ganzfeld experiments published up to that time—forty-two in all—and found that twenty-three experiments in ten different laboratories had hits (instances in which the receiver described and chose the correct picture that was being sent telepathically). This translated into a hit rate of 55 percent—well above what could be explained by chance. However, Ray Hyman, a staunch critic of psi research, disagreed with Honorton's conclusion that the results showed the existence of extrasensory perception. Hyman agreed that the results were an anomaly that needed explanation, but he contended that, allowing for procedural errors, the file drawer problem, and other problems with the experiments, the success rate was closer to 30 percent, not 55 percent. Furthermore, he asserted that after discounting procedural and statistical problems, the results were actually closer to what chance would predict.

Honorton responded to this attack by focusing on just twenty-eight of the forty-two studies that met Hyman's procedural criteria. These studies included 835 separate ganzfeld sessions, with a hit rate of 43 percent. Honorton also broke the experiments down by researcher to show that it was not just one or two experimenters who had such high hit rates. Then he studied how many experiments would have to be hidden in file drawers to lower the hit rate to chance; he discovered that, for every successful study, there would have to be fifteen failed studies that were not published. This meant that there would be 423 ganzfeld experiments (each of which includes dozens or more individual sessions) hidden in file drawers and unknown to the very small population of parapsychologists performing ganzfeld experiments. Hyman eventually agreed that the high hit rate "cannot reasonably be explained by selective reporting or multiple analyses,"[10] although he continued to maintain that the result was due to an unidentifiable flaw in the experiments' procedures.

J.B. Rhine and Zener Cards

Another researcher who had a high hit rate in his psi experiments was J.B. Rhine, a botanist turned parapsychologist.

Rhine developed the Zener cards, a deck of twenty-five cards with five different designs: a star, a cross, a circle, a square, and wavy lines. Rhine's hypothesis was that someone with extrasensory perception should be able to predict which card would be turned up at a rate higher than chance, which is five correct cards in a deck of twenty-five, or 20 percent.

Rhine eventually found someone who appeared to have extraordinary psychic abilities—Hubert E. Pearce Jr. Pearce excelled at predicting the faces on the cards, even when Rhine and the cards were in a different building than Pearce. Pearce normally had between ten and thirteen correct guesses per run of twenty-five cards, an astonishingly high hit rate. Rhine also discovered that psychic ability could be influenced by the subject's moods. Motivated by a reward of $100 per hit, Pearce got every card right in a twenty-five-card run. The odds against such a feat are 298,023,223,876,953,125 to 1. Pearce's psychic ability also dropped when he was tired, bored, or depressed. After his fiancée broke up with him, Pearce's correct guesses dropped considerably. Similarly, Rhine found that psychic ability deteriorated when the subjects were drugged with the barbiturate sodium amytal; psychic ability increased when they were given caffeine.

Rhine and other psychic investigators also discovered that most psychics' abilities declined during periods of extensive testing, a trend known as the decline effect. Some critics claimed that the reason the hit rate declined was due to better controls on the experiments. Rhine argued, however, that these declines in ESP ability show that psychic ability has a natural relationship with physiological and psychological factors; other non-ESP experiments that are dependent on the subjects' motivation also experience a decline effect.

Rhine's critics claimed that forces other than ESP were responsible for the high hit rate in his experiments. Psychologists Leonard Zusne and Warren Jones argued that, in Rhine's early experiments, the subjects could see the cards reflected in the testers' glasses, or, if they did not wear glasses, in their corneas. They also asserted that the cards were so thin that the symbols could be read through the back of the cards, a problem that Rhine soon remedied. Zusne and Jones also maintained that the small screens Rhine erected between the tester and subject were not enough to prevent cheating. They wrote in their critique of his study,

> Changes in facial expression give away clues that are not concealed by small screens. Larger screens still allow the percipient to hear the agent's voice. . . . Voice inflections are as useful a source of information as are facial expressions. Furthermore, the sound of the pen or pencil wielded by the agent as he or she records the calls can be also utilized by a person who is skilled at it or learns the skill when tested over a sufficiently large number of trials. Involuntary whispering on the part of the recording agent cannot be excluded as an additional source of information. When the distance between the percipient and the cards was increased, the scores dropped.[11]

Rhine responded to these allegations by tightening his procedures. He placed his subjects and testers not just in different rooms but in different buildings. His prime subject, Pearce, sat in the library at Duke University while Rhine's assistant, Joseph Pratt, and the Zener cards were in the physics building. The two synchronized their watches, and every minute Pratt would turn over a card and make a note of the card's face, and Pearce would write down his answer. When the session was over, Pratt and Pearce sealed their answers in an envelope before giving them to Rhine to evaluate. The results were amazing: Pearce had a hit rate of nearly 35 percent; he correctly predicted 261 cards out of 750, and in one run, he had thirteen hits.

Still, the biggest criticism of Rhine's research is that few scientists were able to duplicate his results. Theories and hypotheses are generally not accepted by scientists unless the results can be repeated by other researchers, and no one has achieved the same results that Rhine has. Psychologist John Beloff wrote of his experience in testing for psi using Zener cards:

> I recently completed a seven-year programme of parapsychological research with the help of one full time research assistant. No one would have been more delighted to obtain positive results than we, but for all the success we achieved, ESP might just as well not have existed. . . . I have not found on comparing notes with other parapsychologists . . . that my experience is in any way out of the ordinary.[12]

As a consequence of their inability to replicate Rhine's results, many researchers doubt the existence of psi.

Micropsychokinesis

The computer age allowed parapsychologists to develop another experiment to test for psi—the random-number generator (RNG) and the random-event generator (REG). Both machines operate on the same principle: They display numbers or lights randomly and the subjects (operators) try to mentally influence the distribution of numbers or lights. Robert Jahn developed a laboratory at Princeton University to study micropsychokinesis, as the phenomenon is known, as did Helmut Schmidt at Boeing Research Labs in Seattle. Both scientists performed hundreds of thousands of tests, and both achieved results that were statistically significant—high enough over what chance would predict to indicate that psi could be at work.

Critics of the experiments argue that these results are not necessarily the results of psi. Schmidt's results, for example, were only 1 percent higher than chance predicts, which could be significant if they were maintained over thousands of experiments. But these results could also be due to other factors. Victor Stengel discusses one possibility in his book *Physics and Psychics*. While he is careful to not accuse anyone of fraud, he believes that the REGs and RNGs may not be totally random after all:

> Electronic currents are known to "drift." They are often sensitive to heat, shock and humidity. Perhaps the operator noticed a drift over the weeks, and took advantage of it. Perhaps she simply kicked the apparatus, turned it upside down, or blew on some of the transistors.[13]

However, other critics, notably the staunch skeptic Ray Hyman, have noted, "By almost any standard, Schmidt's work is the most challenging ever to confront critics such as myself. His approach makes many of the earlier criticisms of parapsychological research obsolete."[14]

Mediums

Science offers helpful tools to test the claims of many psychics. However, it is much more difficult, if not impossible, to test in the laboratory those who claim they have the ability to contact the dead. Many mediums claim that they do not control the willingness of spirits to talk through them. Furthermore, they also assert that the spirits are less willing to speak when skeptics are near.

For their part, skeptics claim that mediums perform what is known as a "cold reading"; that is, they ask questions of the subjects ("fishing" for information) and pick up on and respond to verbal and nonverbal clues. In other words, most of the information in the reading is provided by the subject, not the medium. The critics assert that mediums make vague comments regarding the deceased, often referring to a month or a number or a letter of the alphabet, knowing that the subject will try to construct some sort of message out of whatever is said. Mediums also know that most people will remember only the hits and forget any incorrect guesses. James Randi, a magician and skeptic, has offered a $1 million reward to any psychic who can prove the existence of his or her powers in a laboratory setting. While the challenge has been accepted several times, no one has ever passed the tests Randi has posed.

Repetition Is Key

Believers and skeptics both point to experiments that succeeded or failed to support their respective point of view. It is important, however, when considering the possibility of psi to consider the whole and not just one example when attempting to prove a position. Hans J. Eysenck and Carl Sargent write in their book *Explaining the Unexplained*,

> It would be wrong to think that such "demonstrations" are necessarily the best evidence for psi. They are only part of the picture. What we really need are *groups of experiments*, reported by different researchers, that show consistent patterns of evidence. Then the accumulation of results—none of which need be overly dramatic taken in isolation—would form a persuasive overall picture. This is a "bundle of sticks" argument. Taken individually, the sticks (individual experiments) may be easy to break. Bound together (considered as groups of related experiments), they cannot be so broken.[15]

One experiment does not prove anything. Only when the tests can be repeated and the same results achieved is it possible to prove—or disprove—a hypothesis. All possible alternatives to psi must be considered. As Theodore Schick Jr. and Lewis Vaughn write in *How to Think About Weird Things*, "Just because you can't explain something doesn't mean it's supernatural."[16]

Notes

1. Quoted in Richard S. Broughton, *Parapsychology: The Controversial Science.* New York: Ballantine Books, 1991, p. 50.
2. Quoted in Broughton, *Parapsychology,* p. 51.

3. Quoted in Theodore Schick Jr. and Lewis Vaughn, *How to Think About Weird Things: Critical Thinking for a New Age.* Mountain View, CA: Mayfield, 1995, p. 13.

4. Quoted in Anthony North, *The Paranormal: A Guide to the Unexplained.* London: Blandford, 1996, p. 156.

5. Broughton, *Parapsychology,* p. 76.

6. Broughton, *Parapsychology,* p. 78.

7. Broughton, *Parapsychology,* p. 78.

8. North, *The Paranormal,* p. 168.

9. Quoted in Time-Life Books, *Psychic Powers.* Alexandria, VA: Time-Life Books, 1987, p. 27.

10. Quoted in Broughton, *Parapsychology,* p. 288.

11. Quoted in Schick and Vaughn, *How to Think About Weird Things,* p. 225.

12. Quoted in Schick and Vaughn, *How to Think About Weird Things,* p. 227.

13. Quoted in Hans J. Eysenck and Carl Sargent, *Explaining the Unexplained: Mysteries of the Paranormal.* London: Prion, 1997, pp. 50–51.

14. Eysenck and Sargent, *Explaining the Unexplained,* p. 45.

15. Eysenck and Sargent, *Explaining the Unexplained,* p. 52.

16. Schick and Vaughn, *How to Think About Weird Things,* p. 20.

Glossary

clairaudient: "Clear hearing," usually meaning that the hearer can hear voices or messages from the dead.

clairsentient: "Clear feeling," the ability to feel the emotions of a spirit.

clairvoyant: "Clear seeing," the extrasensory ability to predict the future; also known as "second sight."

ESP: Extrasensory perception, such as telepathy, clairvoyance, or precognition.

ganzfeld experiment: An experiment in telepathy in which the person receiving the message is placed in a quiet, darkened room, with the eyes covered, and tries to describe a picture sent via psychic means by a sender in another place.

medium: A person who communicates with spirits of the dead; also called a "channeler."

OBE: Out-of-body experience. A feeling of departing one's body and observing it from outside the body.

parapsychology: The scientific study of psychic or paranormal phenomena.

psi (pronounced "sigh"): The term used to indicate both ESP and psychokinesis.

psychic: A person who has paranormal powers, such as ESP, clairvoyance, or psychokinesis.

psychic detective: A psychic who uses paranormal powers to help police solve crimes.

psychic healer/psychic surgeon: A psychic who heals people using paranormal powers. Psychic healers use just the touch of their hands to heal their patients or soothe the energy fields surrounding the patient. Psychic surgeons are reported to make incisions with their fingers and remove diseased organs without any surgical instruments or anesthesia.

psychokinesis: The motion of an object solely by psychic or mental power.

REG: Random-event generator, a computer that randomly activates lightbulbs that are in a circle. It is used in experiments to determine whether a person's mind can influence the pattern of the lights.

remote viewing: The ability to perceive places, people, or time that is not in the range of the five senses.

RNG: Random-number generator, a computer that randomly selects numbers. It is used in experiments to measure whether a person's mind can affect the machine's selection of numbers.

Organizations to Contact

The editors have compiled the following list of organizations concerned with the issues debated in this book. The descriptions are derived from materials provided by the organizations. All have publications or information available for interested readers. The list was compiled on the date of publication of the present volume; names, addresses, phone and fax numbers, and e-mail and Internet addresses may change. Be aware that many organizations take several weeks or longer to respond to inquiries, so allow as much time as possible.

Academy of Religion and Psychical Research
PO Box 614, Bloomfield, CT 06002-0614
(860) 242-4593
e-mail: bateby@infi.net • website: www.lightlink.com

The academy focuses specifically on the area where religion and psychic research interface. It views parapsychology as providing the authoritative model of empirical science and believes it has a bearing on religious claims. It publishes the scholarly quarterly *Journal of Religion and Psychical Research* and the quarterly newsletter *ARPR Bulletin*.

American Association for Parapsychology (AAP)
PO Box 225, Canoga Park, CA 91305
(818) 883-0840 • fax: (818) 884-1850
e-mail: info@parapsychologydegrees.com
website: www.parapsychologydegrees.com

The AAP strives to provide a better understanding of the scientific basis for psychic phenomena and to utilize this knowledge for the betterment of humankind. Through its comprehensive study course on the science of parapsychology, the association attempts to bridge the gap between psychic research in the natural and social sciences and research in philosophy and comparative religion. It publishes the ten-hour audiocassette "A Complete Course in Parapsychology."

American Institute of Parapsychology (AIP)

4131 NW 13th St., Suite 200, Gainesville, FL 32609
(352) 384-0057
e-mail: anichols@citycollege.edu
website: www.afterlife-psychical.org

The purpose of the institute is to provide its members with information to improve their effectiveness as parapsychologists and to educate the public about paranormal aspects of human experience. The AIP is also working to enhance the standing of parapsychology as a science and a profession by establishing standards and procedures to certify that investigators are qualified in parapsychology and paranormal psychology. The institute publishes the quarterly *AIP Journal* and the fact sheets "Channeling and Mediumship" and "After-Death Communication."

American Society for Psychical Research (ASPR)

5 W. 73rd St., New York, NY 10023
(212) 799-5050 • fax: (212) 496-2497
e-mail: aspr@aspr.com • website: www.aspr.com

The ASPR seeks to advance the understanding of psychic phenomena. Through its research and educational programs, the society supports the efforts of both laypersons and professionals to use the study of psychic phenomena to expand and improve the understanding of human nature and the broad scope of human abilities. The ASPR publishes the *ASPR Newsletter* and the *Journal of the American Society for Psychical Research*, both quarterly, as well as numerous books and audio- and videotapes.

Committee for the Scientific Investigation of Claims of the Paranormal (CSICOP)

PO Box 703, Amherst, NY 14226-0703
(716) 636-1425 • fax: (716) 636-1733
e-mail: info@csicop.org • website: www.csicop.org

CSICOP is a scientific and educational organization composed of individuals interested in studying claims of paranormal phenomena. It encourages critical investigation of paranormal and fringe-science claims from a strictly scientific point of view, and disseminates factual information about the results of such inquiries to the scientific community and the public. CSICOP publishes the bimonthly magazine *Skeptical Inquirer* and the quarterly newsletter *Skeptical Briefs*.

Mind Development and Control Association
9633 Cinnabar Dr., Sappington, MO 63126
(314) 849-3722

The association develops and promotes interest in various facets of paranormal and psychic research. It provides monthly correspondence lessons in psychic arts and sciences as well as classes in psychic development and ESP skills. The association publishes the *U.S. Psi Squad*.

Parapsychology Foundation
228 E. 71st St., New York, NY 10021
(212) 628-1550 • fax: (212) 628-1559
e-mail: info@parapsychology.org
website: www.parapsychology.org

The foundation was established in 1951 to promote and support impartial scientific inquiry into the psychic aspects of human nature. It encourages scientific investigators to pursue independent studies of the human mind, and it acts as a clearinghouse for parapsychological information. The foundation publishes the book *Guide to Sources of Information on Parapsychology*, the pamphlet *Introduction to Parapsychology*, and the *International Journal of Parapsychology*, which is published twice a year.

Rhine Research Center
Institute for Parapsychology
402 N. Buchanan Blvd., Durham, NC 27701-1728
(919) 688-8241 • fax: (919) 683-4338
e-mail: info@rhine.org • website: www.rhine.org

The center is a research and educational organization established to explore unusual types of experiences that suggest capabilities yet unrecognized in the realm of human personality. It seeks to bridge gaps between the academic community and independent researchers and between the general public and the research laboratory. The center publishes the quarterly *Journal of Parapsychology*.

Skeptics Society
PO Box 338, Altadena, CA 91001
(626) 794-3119 • fax: (626) 794-1301
e-mail: skepticmag@aol.com • website: www.skeptic.com

The society is composed of scholars, scientists, and historians who promote the use of scientific methods to scrutinize such nonscientific traditions as religion, superstition, mysticism, and New Age beliefs. It is devoted to the investigation of extraordinary claims and revolutionary ideas and to the promotion of science and critical thinking. The society publishes the quarterly *Skeptic Magazine* and the pamphlet *The Baloney Detection Kit*.

Society for Scientific Exploration (SSE)
PO Box 3818, Charlottesville, VA 22903
fax: (804) 924-3104
website: www.scientificexploration.org

Affiliated with the University of Virginia's Department of Astronomy, the society seeks to provide a professional forum for presentations, criticisms, and debates concerning topics that are ignored or given inadequate study by mainstream academia. It wants to increase understanding of the factors that at present limit the scope of scientific inquiry. The society publishes the quarterlies *Journal of Scientific Exploration* and *Explorer* newsletter. The journal is available from PO Box 5848, Stanford, CA 94309-5848.

Survival Research Foundation (SRF)
PO Box 63-0026, Miami, FL 33163-0026
(305) 936-1408

The SRF searches for valid evidence of postmortem survival and communication. It conducts research on near-death experiences and presents the results to universities and the public through publications and lectures. Among the foundation's publications are the *Encyclopedia of Parapsychology and Psychical Research* and the papers "Death Comes Alive" and "Tests for Communication with the Dead."

Western Canada Skeptics Societies

Alberta Skeptics
Box 5571, Station A, Calgary, Alberta T2H 1X9
e-mail: abskeptics@hotmail.com
website: http://abskeptic.htmlplanet.com

British Columbia Skeptics
c/o Lee Moller, 1188 Beaufort Rd., Vancouver, BC V7G 1R7
website: http://psg.com

Manitoba Skeptics
Box 92, St. Vital, Winnipeg, Manitoba R2M 4A5

The three Western Canada Skeptics Societies are resource and educational centers for schools, media, and others interested in paranormal phenomena. Their members use the scientific method to investigate claims of paranormal phenomena. The organizations jointly publish the quarterly publication *Rational Enquirer*.

For Further Research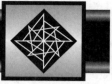

Books

Richard S. Broughton, *Parapsychology: The Controversial Science.* New York: Ballantine Books, 1991.

Sylvia Browne with Lindsay Harrison, *Life on the Other Side: A Psychic's Tour of the Afterlife.* New York: Dutton, 2000.

Edgar Cayce, *My Life as a Seer: The Lost Memoirs.* Compiled and edited by Robert A. Smith. New York: St. Martin's Press, 1997.

John Edward, *One Last Time: A Psychic Medium Speaks to Those We Have Loved and Lost.* New York: Berkley, 1998.

Hans J. Eysenck and Carl Sargent, *Explaining the Unexplained: Mysteries of the Paranormal.* London: Prion, 1997.

Kendrick Frazier, ed., *Encounters with the Paranormal: Science, Knowledge, and Belief.* Amherst, NY: Prometheus, 1998.

John Friedlander and Gloria Hemsher, *Basic Psychic Development: A User's Guide to Auras, Chakras, and Clairvoyance.* York Beach, ME: Samuel Weiser, 1999.

Fred M. Frohock, *Lives of the Psychics: The Shared Worlds of Science and Mysticism.* Chicago: University of Chicago Press, 2000.

Dale E. Graff, *Tracks in the Psychic Wilderness: An Exploration of ESP, Remote Viewing, Precognitive Dreaming, and Synchronicity.* Boston: Element, 1998.

Elmar R. Gruber, *Psychic Wars: Parapsychology in Espionage—and Beyond.* London: Blandford, 1999.

Valerie Hope and Maurice Townsend, eds., *The Paranormal Investigator's Handbook*. London: Collins and Brown, 1999.

Nicholas Humphrey, *Leaps of Faith: Science, Miracles, and the Search for Supernatural Consolation*. New York: Copernicus, 1999.

H.J. Irwin, *An Introduction to Parapsychology*. 3rd ed. Jefferson, NC: McFarland, 1998.

Stephen Jones, ed., *Dancing with the Dark: True Encounters with the Paranormal by Masters of the Macabre*. New York: Carroll and Graf, 1999.

W. Adam Mandelbaum, *The Psychic Battlefield: A History of the Military-Occult Complex*. New York: St. Martin's Press, 2000.

Jonathan Margolis, *Uri Geller: Magician or Mystic?* New York: Welcome Rain, 1999.

David Marks, *The Psychology of the Psychic*. 2nd ed. Amherst, NY: Prometheus, 2000.

Joanne D.S. McMahon and Anna M. Lascurain, *Shopping for Miracles: A Guide to Psychics and Psychic Powers*. Lincolnwood, IL: Lowell House, 1997.

Joseph McMoneagle, *Mind Trek*. 2nd ed. Charlottesville, VA: Hampton Roads, 1997.

———, *Remote Viewing Secrets: A Handbook*. Charlottesville, VA: Hampton Roads, 2000

David Morehouse, *Psychic Warrior: Inside the CIA's Stargate Program: The True Story of a Soldier's Espionage and Awakening*. New York: St. Martin's Press, 1996.

Belleruth Naparstek, *Your Sixth Sense: Activating Your Psychic Potential*. San Francisco: HarperSanFrancisco, 1997.

Anthony North, *The Paranormal: A Guide to the Unexplained*. London: Blandford, 1996.

Dean Radin, *The Conscious Universe: The Scientific Truth of Psychic Phenomena*. San Francisco: HarperEdge, 1997.

Andrei Ridgeway, *Psychic Living: Tap into Your Psychic Potential*. New York: Kensington Books, 1999.

Lynn A. Robinson and LaVonne Carlson-Finnerty, *The Complete Idiot's Guide to Being Psychic*. New York: Alpha Books, 1999.

Theodore Schick Jr. and Lewis Vaughn, *How to Think About Weird Things: Critical Thinking for a New Age*. Mountain View, CA: Mayfield, 1995.

Charles E. Sellier and Joe Meier, *The Paranormal Sourcebook: A Comprehensive Guide to All Things Otherworldly*. Lincolnwood, IL: Lowell House, 1999.

Michael Shermer, *Why People Believe Weird Things: Pseudoscience, Superstition, and Other Confusions of Our Time*. New York: W.H. Freeman, 1997.

Jess Stearn, *Edgar Cayce: The Sleeping Prophet: The Life, the Prophecies, and Readings of America's Most Famous Mystic*. Virginia Beach, VA: A.R.E. Press, 1996.

Douglas M. Stokes, *The Nature of Mind: Parapsychology and the Role of Consciousness in the Physical World*. Jefferson, NC: McFarland, 1997.

Russell Targ and Jane Katra, *Miracles of Mind: Exploring Nonlocal Consciousness and Spiritual Healing*. Novato, CA: New World Library, 1998.

Time-Life Books, *Psychic Powers*. Alexandria, VA: Time-Life Books, 1987.

Richard Wiseman, *Deception and Self-Deception: Investigating Psychics*. Amherst, NY: Prometheus, 1997.

Periodicals

Daniel Akst, "Forget What Psychics See. At Least They Listen," *New York Times*, February 6, 2000.

Stephen Barr, "The Case of the Psychic Sleuth," *Good Housekeeping*, March 1997.

Don Barry, "The NYPD's Psychic Friend," *New York Times*, July 21, 1997.

Daryl J. Bem, John Palmer, and Richard S. Broughton, "Updating the Ganzfeld Database: A Victim of Its Own Success?" *Journal of Parapsychology*, September 2001.

Nina Bernstein, "On Welfare and Not Clairvoyant? New York Will Provide Training," *New York Times*, January 28, 2000.

Frank Bruni, "Your Future Is Very Clear. You Will Be Paying a Bill," *New York Times*, August 24, 1997.

Siri Carpenter, "ESP Findings Send Controversial Message," *Science News*, July 31, 1999.

Christina Boyle Cush and Sophie Sjoholm, "Can a Psychic Change Your Life?" *Redbook*, September 2000.

Deborah Gregory, "The Skeptic and the Psychics," *Essence*, October 1996.

Ray Hyman, "The Evidence for Psychic Functioning: Claims vs. Reality," *Skeptical Inquirer*, March/April 1996.

Leon Jaroff, "Talking to the Dead," *Time*, March 5, 2001.

Jeffrey Kluger, "CIA ESP," *Discover*, April 1996.

Paul Kurtz, "The New Paranatural Paradigm: Claims of Communicating with the Dead," *Skeptical Inquirer*, November/ December 2000.

———, "The New Skepticism," *Skeptical Briefs*, June 1998. Available from PO Box 703, Amherst, NY 14226-0703.

Nadya Labi, "I See a Policeman in Your Future," *Time*, February 22, 1999.

Ruth LaFerla, "A Voice from the Other Side," *New York Times*, October 29, 2000.

Caroline Leavitt, "My Best Friend Is a Psychic," *Redbook*, October 1999.

Nicole Lundrigan, "Perception Without Sensation: Looking at ESP," *Odyssey*, December 2000.

Merrill Markoe, "Desperately Seeking a Psychic," *American Health*, October 1996.

Edwin C. May, "The American Institutes for Research Review of the Department of Defense's Stargate Program: A Commentary," *Journal of Parapsychology*, March 1996.

Ellen Michaud, "This Woman Says She Can Feel Your Pain . . . and Heal You," *Prevention*, September 1999.

Kenneth Miller and Harry Benson, "Psychics: Science or Séance?" *Life*, June 1998.

Julie Milton and Richard Wiseman, "A Meta-Analysis of Mass-Media Tests of Extrasensory Perception," *British Journal of Psychology*, May 1999. Available at http://giorgio. catchword.com.

Jill Neimark, "Do the Spirits Move You?" *Psychology Today*, September 19, 1996.

Joe Nickell, "Investigating Spirit Communications," *Skeptical Briefs*, September 1998.

Judith Orloff and Sherry Suib Cohen, "Are You Psychic?" *McCall's*, March 1997.

Gary Posner and Wallace Sampson, "Chinese Acupuncture for Heart Surgery Anesthesia," *Scientific Review of Alternative Medicine*, Fall/Winter 1999. Available from 59 John Glenn Dr., Amherst, NY 14228-2197.

Benjamin Radford, "The Ten-Percent Myth," *Skeptical Inquirer*, March/April 1999.

Jeanie Russell, "The 'Doctors' Who Feel Your Pain," *Good Housekeeping*, July 1998.

Rochelle Jewel Shapiro, "The Medium Has a Message," *New York Times Magazine*, March 28, 1999.

Michael Shermer, "Deconstructing the Dead," *Scientific American*, August 2001.

Peter Sturrock, "Curious, Creative, and Critical Thinking," *Truth Seeker*, vol. 124, no. 1, 1997. Available from PO Box 28550, San Diego, CA 92198.

Richard Webster, "Psychic Animals," *Fate*, May 2000. Available from PO Box 1940, Marion, OH 43305-1940.

Steven R. Wills, "'Cold' Reading," *Odyssey*, December 2000.

Index